Th

"I have been keeping an eye on Bunin's brilliant
talent. He really is the enemy."
Andrei Bely

"Your influence is truly beyond words… I do not know any other
writer whose external world is so closely tied
to another, whose sensations are more exact and indispensable
and whose world is more genuine and
also more unexpected than yours."
André Gide

"He was a great stylist who wrote very suggestively.
He didn't spray us with ideologies or worries.
His writing is pure poetry."
Andrei Makine

"A most powerful 'connoisseur of colours'. One could write an
entire dissertation on his colour schemes."
Vladimir Nabokov

"You have, Mr Bunin, thoroughly explored the
soul of vanished Russia, and in doing so you have
most deservedly continued the glorious traditions
of the great Russian literature."
Professor Wilhelm Nordenson,
at the 1933 Nobel Prize banquet

Contents

Ivan Bunin (1870–1953)

The Village

1

THE KRASOVS' GREAT-GRANDFATHER, nicknamed Gypsy by the servants, had borzoi hounds set on him by his master, Durnovo. Gypsy had stolen his lover from him, his master. Durnovo ordered Gypsy to be taken out into the fields beyond Durnovka and sat on a knoll. He himself rode out with the pack, crying: "Tally-ho!" Gypsy, who had been sitting benumbed, made off at a run. But you shouldn't run away from borzois.

The Krasovs' grandfather was lucky enough to win his freedom. He left with his family for the town and soon made a name for himself: he became a renowned thief. He rented a shack in the Chornaya Sloboda for his wife and he settled her down to make lace to sell, while he himself, with a poor townsman, Belokopytov, went off around the province robbing churches. When he was caught, he conducted himself in such a way that for a long time people throughout the district were enraptured by him – he stands there, apparently, in a velveteen kaftan and goatskin boots with his cheekbones and eyes playing brazenly, and confesses most deferentially to even the very least of his countless jobs:

"Yes, sir. Yes, sir."

And the Krasovs' father was a small-time trader. He travelled around the district, lived at one time in his native Durnovka, and tried setting up a store there, but he went bust, turned to drink, went back to town and died. After working in stores, his sons, Tikhon and Kuzma, were in trade as well. They used to drag along in a cart with a locker in the middle and yell out dolefully:

"La-adies, wa-ares! La-adies, wa-ares!"

The wares – little mirrors, soaps, rings, cottons, kerchiefs, needles, pretzels – were in the locker. And in the cart was everything they got in exchange for the wares: dead cats, eggs, homespun canvas, old clothes...

But one day, after travelling for several years, the brothers almost knifed one another – and they parted, so as not to tempt fate. Kuzma

3

got a job with a cattle-dealer, Tikhon rented a little inn on the highway at the station of Vorgol, some five *versts** from Durnovka, and opened a tavern and a "taxable" store:* "trading in generel goods tea shoogar tabacco sigarets et setera".

By the age of about forty, Tikhon's beard was already silvery in places. But he was handsome, tall and slim, as before; stern of face, swarthy, a little pockmarked, broad in the shoulder and wiry, masterful and abrupt in his conversation, quick and agile in his movements. Only his brows had begun knitting ever more frequently, and his eyes flashing ever more sharply than before.

Tirelessly he would chase after the district policemen in those dark days of autumn when they exact taxes and sale after sale takes place in the village. Tirelessly he would buy up standing crops from landowners and rent land for a song... He lived for a long time with a mute cook – "it's no bad thing, she can't go spreading any gossip!" – and had a child with her, which she took into her bed and crushed in her sleep, and then he married a middle-aged housemaid of old Princess Shakhova's. And after marrying and getting the dowry, he "finished off" the heir of the now impoverished Durnovo family, a plump, delicate young gentleman, bald at twenty-five, but with a magnificent chestnut-coloured beard. And the peasants just gasped in pride when he took over the Durnovo family's small estate: after all, practically the whole of Durnovka was made up of Krasovs!

They gasped too at the way he contrived to be everywhere at once: selling, buying, on the estate almost every day, watching like a hawk over every speck of land... They gasped and said:

"He's a brute! He's the boss, though!"

Tikhon Ilyich himself persuaded them of this. He would often say edifyingly:

"We're careful and we get along – catch you and we'll put the bridle on. But justly so. I'm a Russian, brother. I don't want anything of yours for nothing, but you bear it in mind: I'm damned if I'll let you have a kopek of mine! Mollycoddle you – no, mark my words, that I won't!"

And Nastasya Petrovna (yellow, swollen, with sparse, whitish hair, who, because of her continual pregnancies, always ending with still-born girls, walked like a duck, with her toes pointing inwards and rocking from side to side) would groan as she listened:

"Oh, what a simpleton, just look at you! Why take such trouble with him, the stupid thing? You try teaching him good sense, but nothing's any use. Look at him standing with his legs apart – like some bukhara from Emir!"*

In the autumn, beside the inn, which stood with one side facing the highway and the other facing the station and the grain-elevator, there was the moaning and groaning of creaking wheels: strings of carts filled with grain were swinging round from both up the road and down. And pulleys were constantly squealing, now on the door to the tavern, where Nastasya Petrovna was serving, now on the door to the store – dark, dirty, smelling strongly of soap, herring, cheap tobacco, mint cake and paraffin. And ringing out constantly in the tavern was:

"Oo-ooph! That vodka of yours is strong stuff, Petrovna! Gave me a whack right in the forehead, the devil take it."

"Like sugar on your lips, my dear!"

"Put snuff in it, do you?"

"Don't be such an idiot!"

And the store was even busier:

"Ilyich! Can you weigh me out a pount of ham?"

"This year, brother, thanks be to God, I've got such a supply of ham, such a supply!"

"And how much is it?"

"Dirt cheap!"

"Storekeeper! Have you got any good tar?"

"Your grandfather never had such tar at his wedding, my dear!"

"And how much is it?"

The loss of hope of having children and the closing down of the taverns were the major events in Tikhon Ilyich's life. He aged visibly when there was no longer any doubt that he wasn't to be a father. At first he joked about it:

"No, sir, I shall get what I want," he would say to acquaintances. "A man isn't a man without children. Just like some barren patch of ground…"

Then he even began to be gripped by fear: what's going on – one's crushed a child in bed, the other keeps giving birth to dead ones! And the time of Nastasya Petrovna's final pregnancy was an especially difficult one. Tikhon Ilyich was miserable, in a bad temper; Nastasya Petrovna prayed in secret, cried in secret, and she was pitiful when, by

5

the light of the icon lamp, she would climb down quietly from the bed at night, thinking her husband was asleep, and start laboriously getting down on her knees, bowing to the floor with a whisper, looking up in anguish at the icons and rising agonizingly from her knees like an old woman. From childhood, without even daring to admit it to himself, Tikhon Ilyich had disliked icon lamps, their false church light: there had remained in his memory all his life that November night when, in the tiny, lop-sided shack in the Chornaya Sloboda, an icon lamp had been burning too – so meekly, gently and sadly – the shadows from its chains had been dark, it had been deathly quiet, and on the bench beneath the saints his father had lain motionless with his eyes closed, his sharp nose raised and his waxen hands clasped on his breast, while near to him, beyond the little window, curtained with a red cloth, some conscripts had been passing by with wildly melancholy songs, wailing, and concertinas bawling out of tune... Now the icon lamp burned constantly.

Some hawkers from Vladimir fed their horses at the inn – and in the house there appeared *The New Complete Oracle and Wizard, foretelling the future from questions posed, with in addition The easiest method of fortune-telling with cards, beans and coffee.* And in the evenings, Nastasya Petrovna would put on her glasses, roll herself a little ball of wax, and begin tossing it onto the rings of the oracle. And Tikhon Ilyich would throw sidelong glances. But all the answers given were crude, ominous or senseless.

"'Does my husband love me?'" asked Nastasya Petrovna.

And the oracle replied:

"'He loves you like a dog loves a stick.'"

"'How many children will I have?'"

"'Fate has doomed you to die, the field must be rid of its weeds.'"

Then Tikhon Ilyich said:

"Let me toss it..."

And asked the question:

"'Should I instigate a lawsuit against the person concerned?'"

But he too got nonsense back:

"'Count the teeth in your mouth.'"

Once, glancing into the otherwise empty kitchen, Tikhon Ilyich saw his wife beside the cook's child's cradle. A speckled chick was wandering along the window sill, cheeping and tapping its beak against the glass

6

as it caught flies, while she was sitting on the plank bed, rocking the cradle and singing an old lullaby in a pitiful, tremulous voice:

Where lies my little baby?
Where now his tiny bed?
He's in a lofty tower,
In a cradle painted bright.
No one come to visit us,
No, knock not at the tower!
His eyes are closed, he's fast asleep
Behind a dark bed curtain
Of richly coloured taffeta...

And Tikhon Ilyich's face was so changed at that moment that, when she glanced at him, Nastasya Petrovna was not embarrassed and did not quail – she just burst into tears and, blowing her nose, said quietly:

"For Christ's sake, take me to the saint..."

And Tikhon Ilyich took her to Zadonsk. On the way, he was thinking God ought to punish him all the same for the fact that in his hustle and bustle he was only to be found in church at Easter. And blasphemous thoughts came into his head too: he kept comparing himself with the parents of saints who had also gone a long time without having children. This was not a clever thing to do, but he had already noticed long before that there was someone else inside him, stupider than he. Just before setting off he had received a letter from Athos: "*Most God-fearing benefactor Tikhon Ilyich! Peace and salvation to you, the Lord's blessing and the honest Protection of the All-glorified Mother of God from Her earthly lot, the holy Mount Athos! I had the happiness of hearing of your good deeds and of how you lovingly spare mites for the creation and decoration of God's temples and for monastic cells. My hut through time has now reached such a state of dilapidation...*" And Tikhon Ilyich had sent a tenner for repairs to the hut. The time had long gone when he had believed with naive pride that word of him really had reached Athos itself, he knew very well now that there were simply too many huts on Athos that had fallen into disrepair – and he had sent it all the same. But still it didn't help, the pregnancy ended with utter torment: before giving birth to a last stillborn child, Nastasya Petrovna, while falling asleep, began shuddering, groaning, screaming...

7

According to her, she was instantly gripped in her sleep by a kind of wild gaiety, combined with inexpressible terror: first she would see the Queen of Heaven coming towards her through the fields, all aglow with golden raiments, and from somewhere would come harmonious, ever swelling singing; then from underneath the bed would leap a little devil, indistinguishable from the darkness, yet clearly visible to her inner eye, and start belting something out on a harmonica in such a resonant, jaunty, boisterous way! It would have been easier to sleep not in the stuffy heat, on feather mattresses, but in the fresh air, under the overhang of the granaries. But Nastasya Petrovna was afraid:

"The dogs'll come up and sniff around my head…"

When all hope of having children had gone, the thought occurred to him ever more frequently: "Who's all this torment for, then, the devil take it?" And the state monopoly was rubbing salt in the wound. His hands started to shake, his brows to knit and rise as if in pain, his lip to twist – especially at the phrase which was always on his tongue: "bear it in mind". He tried as before to look younger than he was – he wore foppish calfskin boots and an embroidered *kosovorotka** under a double-breasted jacket. But his beard grew greyer, and thinner, and tangled…

And as if on purpose, the summer turned out hot and droughty. The rye failed completely. And complaining to customers became something to enjoy.

"We're closing down, sir, closing down!" Tikhon Ilyich would say with joy of his trade in alcohol, rapping out every syllable. "What else! The state monopoly! The Minister of Finance fancies doing some selling himself!"

"Oh, just look at you!" groaned Nastasya Petrovna. "You'll say too much one day, you will! They'll send you where the raven never took any bones!"

"You can't scare me!" Tikhon Ilyich would cut her off, raising his brows abruptly. "No, sir! You can't put a gag on every mouth!"

And enunciating the words even more sharply, he would turn again to the customer:

"And the rye simply fills you with joy, sir! Bear it in mind: fills everyone with joy! Even in the night, sir – you can see it. You go out onto the doorstep, look into the moonlit fields: nothing there, sir, like a bald patch! You go out and look: it's all shimmering!"

That year, during the fast before Peter and Paul's Day,* Tikhon Ilyich spent four days in town at the fair and got even more upset – by his thoughts, the heat, sleepless nights. He usually set off for the fair with great enthusiasm. They would oil the carts in the twilight and fill them up with hay; into the one in which the master himself and his old workman were riding they put pillows and a *chuika*.* They would start out late at night and drag along, creaking, until dawn. At first they enjoyed friendly conversation, they smoked and told each other scary old stories about merchants murdered on the road and during overnight stops; then Tikhon Ilyich would settle down to sleep – and it was so pleasant hearing the voices of oncoming people in his sleep, feeling the cart rocking shakily and seeming to be forever going downhill, his cheek shifting about on the pillow, his cap falling off and the freshness of the night cooling his head; it was good too waking up before the sun on a pink dewy morning amidst matt-green crops, and catching sight in the distance of the cheerful whiteness of the town in the blue lowland, the gleam of its churches, and having a good yawn, crossing himself at the sound of distant bells and taking the reins from the hands of the sleepy old man, grown weak like a child in the morning chill, and pale as chalk in the light of the sunrise... Now Tikhon Ilyich sent the carts off with the foreman, and he himself travelled alone in a cabriolet. The night was warm and light, but nothing brought him any joy; the journey made him tired; the lights at the fair, in the jail and the hospital, which stood at the entrance to the town, could be seen for about ten *versts* across the steppe, and it seemed as if you would never reach them, those distant, sleepy lights. And it was so hot at the inn on Schepnaya Square, and the bedbugs bit so hard, and so frequently did voices ring out by the gates, such a clatter did the carts driving into the stone yard make, and so early did the cocks begin yelling and the pigeons cooing, and the pale light appear outside the open windows, that he got not a wink of sleep. He slept but little on the second night too, which he tried spending at the fair, in a cart: horses neighed, lights burned in tents, people walked and talked all around, and at dawn, when his eyelids were simply sticking together, bells started ringing in the jail and the hospital – and a cow set up an awful bellowing just above his head...

"Torment!" constantly came to mind during those days and nights.

The fair, sprawling over the common for an entire *verst*, was, as always, noisy and chaotic. There was a discordant hubbub – the neighing of horses, the trills of children's whistles, the marches and polkas of the orchestrions crashing out on the carousels. A garrulous crowd of peasants, men and women, thronged from morning till evening down the dusty, dung-strewn lanes between the carts and tents, horses and cows, booths and food stalls, from which came the stinking fumes of greasy braziers. As always, there were swarms of horse-dealers, imparting terrible heat to every argument and deal; stretching out in endless lines with their nasal refrains were the blind and the poor, beggars and cripples, on crutches and trolleys; moving slowly in the midst of the crowd with its little bells ringing was the police chief's troika, held in check by a coachman in a velveteen, sleeveless jacket and a little hat with peacock feathers... Tikhon Ilyich had a lot of customers. He was approached by black-haired gypsies, ginger-haired Polish Jews in canvas overalls and worn-down boots, tanned landowners in *poddyovkas** and caps; he was approached by a handsome hussar, Prince Bakhtin, and his wife in an English suit, and by an ancient hero of Sebastopol, Khvostov – tall and bony, with amazing large features on his dark, wrinkled face, in a long uniform coat and sagging trousers, boots with wide toes and a big cap with a yellow band, from beneath which his hair, dyed a dead brown colour, was combed forwards onto his temples... Bakhtin, as he looked at a horse, leant back, gave a restrained smile into his moustache and tiny beard, and fidgeted with his leg in cherry-coloured breeches. Khvostov, after shuffling up to a horse which looked at him sidelong with a fiery eye, would stop in such a way that he seemed to be falling over, would raise a crutch and ask for the tenth time in a muffled, expressionless voice:

"How much are you asking?"

And everyone had to be answered. And Tikhon Ilyich did answer, but only with an effort, clenching his jaws, and he would demand such high prices that everyone went away with nothing.

He got very tanned, grew thinner and wan, got dusty, and felt mortal anguish and weakness throughout his body. He upset his stomach so much that he began having spasms. He was obliged to go to the hospital. But there he waited his turn for about two hours, sat in an echoing corridor sniffing the disagreeable smell of carbolic acid, and felt as though he were not Tikhon Ilyich, but were in the antechamber of his master or his superior. And when a heavy-breathing doctor,

10

looking like a deacon, red-faced, light-eyed, in a black frockcoat that was too tight for him and smelt of copper, put his cold ear up against his chest, he hastened to say that his stomach was "almost better", and only out of timidity did he not refuse castor oil. And returning to the fair, he swallowed down a glass of vodka with pepper and salt, and again began eating sausage and poor-quality bread, drinking tea, unboiled water, sour cabbage soup – but still he was unable to quench his thirst. Acquaintances invited him to "refresh himself with some beer" – and he went. The *kvas** seller yelled:

"Have some *kvas*, it's a kick in a glass! A kopek a time, the number one lemonade!"

And he stopped the *kvas* seller.

"He-ere's ice cream!" cried the tenor voice of a bald, sweating ice-cream seller, a fat-bellied old man in a red shirt.

And from an ivory spoon he ate ice cream that was almost like snow, which made for a cruel ache in the temples.

The dusty common, pounded by feet, wheels and hoofs, and strewn with litter and dung, was already emptying – the fair was dispersing. But as if to spite somebody, Tikhon Ilyich continued to keep the unsold horses in the heat and the dust, continued to sit on the cart. Good Lord, what a land! Black earth an *arshin** and a half deep, and what earth! But not five years go by without a famine. The town is famed throughout Russia for its trade in grain – but only a hundred people in the whole town have enough of that grain to eat. And the fair itself? Beggars, simpletons, blind men, cripples – and all the kind that make you feel scared and wretched just looking at them – a whole regiment of them!

Tikhon Ilyich drove home on a hot, sunny morning along the Old Highway. He drove first through the town and the market, then across the shallow little river, soured by the leatherworks, and, beyond the river, uphill, through the Chornaya Sloboda. He had once worked at the market, along with his brother, in Matorin's store. Now everyone at the market bowed to him. His childhood had passed in the Sloboda – on this hillock, amidst sunken daub huts with rotten, blackened roofs, amidst the dung that they dry in front of them for fuel, amidst rubbish, cinders and rags... There was no trace now of the hut where Tikhon Ilyich had been born and grown up. In its place stood a new little plank-built house with a rusty sign over the entrance:

"Ecclesiastical Tailor Sobolev". Everything else in the Sloboda was as it had been: pigs and chickens beside the doorsteps; tall poles by the gates, and sheep's horns on the poles; the large, pale faces of lace-makers peering out from behind pots of flowers through tiny little windows; barefooted little boys with one brace over their shoulders flying a paper kite with a bast tail; quiet, tow-haired little girls by the *zavalinkas** playing their favourite game – dolls' funerals... At the top of the hill, amidst fields, he crossed himself in the direction of the graveyard, behind whose fence, amongst old trees, there had once been the terrifying grave of the wealthy skinflint Zykov, which had fallen in at the very moment they had finished filling it up. And after giving it some thought, he turned the horse towards the gates of the graveyard.

By those big, white gates sat an old woman knitting a stocking, and looking like an old woman from a fairytale – with glasses, with a beak, with sunken lips – one of the widows who lived in the almshouse at the graveyard.

"Hello, granny!" cried Tikhon Ilyich, tying the horse to a pillar by the gates. "Can you look after my horse?"

The old woman stood up, bowed low and mumbled:

"I can, sir."

Tikhon Ilyich took off his cap, rolled his eyes up towards his forehead and crossed himself once more in the direction of the painting of the Assumption of the Virgin above the gates, and added:

"Are there many of you here now?"

"A full dozen old women, sir."

"Well, and do you argue a lot?"

"We do, sir..."

And Tikhon Ilyich set off unhurriedly between trees and crosses down the path leading to the old wooden church. At the fair he had had his hair cut, his beard evened up and shortened – and he looked much younger. He was made to look younger by his thinness after the illness. He was made to look younger by his tan – only the trimmed triangles on his temples had the whiteness of delicate skin. He was made to look younger by his memories of childhood and youth, and by his new canvas cap. He walked and gazed from side to side... How short and muddled life is! And what peace and quiet all around in this sunny calm, inside the fence of the old cemetery! A hot wind was

12

rushing through the tops of the light trees, thinned out prematurely by the intense heat and allowing the cloudless sky to show through, and it swung their transparent, light shade over the stones and the monuments. And when it dropped, the hot sun warmed the flowers and grasses, the birds in the bushes sang sweetly, and the butterflies, in sweet languor, were dead still on the hot pathways... On one cross Tikhon Ilyich read:

> What dreadful quit-rents
> Death gathers from men!

But there was nothing dreadful around him. He walked, remarking even with a sort of pleasure that the graveyard was growing, that a lot of new mausoleums had appeared among the ancient gravestones in the form of coffins on legs, of heavy, cast-iron slabs, and of huge, crude, already rotting crosses, of which it was full. "Passed away on 7th November 1819 at five in the morning" – such inscriptions were terrible to read: death at the dawn of an inclement autumn day in an old provincial town is not a nice thing! But nearby, between the trees, shone the whiteness of a plaster angel with its eyes fixed upon the sky, and hammered out in golden letters on the plinth beneath it was: "Blessed are the dead that die in the Lord!" On the iron monument of some Collegiate Assessor,* made iridescent by bad weather and time, could be made out the verses:

> He served the Tsar most honestly,
> He loved his neighbour heartily,
> Was honoured by his fellow men...

Those verses seemed false to Tikhon Ilyich. But – where is the truth? A human jawbone is lying about here in the bushes, looking as if it were made of dirty wax – all that remains of a man... But is it all? Flowers, ribbons, crosses, coffins and bones in the ground are rotting – all is death and decay! But Tikhon Ilyich walked on and read: "So also is the resurrection of the dead. It is sown in corruption; it is raised in incorruption."*

All the inscriptions spoke touchingly of quiet and rest, of tenderness, of a love which seemingly does not and will not exist on earth, of people's devotion to one another and obedience to God, of those fervent hopes for a future life and a reunion in another, blessed land, in all of which you believe only here, and of the equality which death alone brings – those moments when the dead beggar is kissed on the lips in a final kiss as a brother, and is made the equal of tsars and bishops... And there, inside the furthest corner of the fence, in elder bushes slumbering in the full heat of the sun, Tikhon Ilyich caught sight of a fresh, child's grave, a cross, and on the cross a couplet:

> quiet, leaves, now not one peep,
> let my Kostya stay asleep!

– and, remembering his own child, crushed in its sleep by the mute cook, he began to blink at the tears that welled up.

No one ever rides along the highway that leads past the graveyard and disappears amidst undulating fields. They ride along the dusty cart track beside it. Tikhon Ilyich set off along the cart track too. Towards him rushed a peeling hire cab – provincial cab-drivers really get a move on! – and in the cab was a man from town out hunting: at his feet was a skewbald pointer, on his knees – a gun in a case, on his feet – high marsh waders, though there were no marshes whatsoever in the district. And Tikhon Ilyich clenched his teeth angrily: he'd like to see this loafer as a workman. The midday sun was scorching, the hot wind was blowing, the cloudless sky was becoming slate-coloured. And ever more angrily did Tikhon Ilyich turn away from the dust flying along the road, ever more anxiously did he squint at the scrawny crops, drying out prematurely.

At a measured pace, with tall staffs, walked crowds of female pilgrims, worn out with tiredness and the intense heat. They made low, humble bows to Tikhon Ilyich, but everything already seemed like falsity to him again now:

"So humble! But I bet they scrap like dogs when they stop for the night!"

Some drunken peasants returning from the fair were driving their wretched horses on, raising clouds of dust – they were ginger, greying, black-haired, but all equally ugly, scrawny and ragged. And overtaking their rattling carts, Tikhon Ilyich shook his head:

"Ugh, vagrants, the devil take you!"

One, wearing a cotton shirt that was ripped to shreds, was lying on his back asleep, rocking about like a dead man, with his head thrown back and his bloodied beard and swollen nose sticking up, covered in dried blood. Another was running to try and catch up with the hat that had been torn off by the wind; he stumbled, and with malicious pleasure Tikhon Ilyich walloped him with his knout. He came upon a cart filled with sieves, spades and peasant women; sitting with their backs to the horse, they shook and bumped up and down; one had a new child's cap on her head with the peak at the back, another was singing, a third was waving her arms and yelling after Tikhon Ilyich with roars of laughter:

"Mister! You've lost your linchpin!"

And he held back his horse, allowed himself to be overtaken and walloped the woman with his knout as well.

Beyond the town gates, where the highway turned aside, where the rattling carts fell behind, and quietness, the space and heat of the steppe took hold, he again felt that the main thing in the world was, after all, "business". Oh, what poverty there was all around! The peasants were completely destitute, there wasn't a silver kopek left in the depleted little estates scattered around the district... A firm hand was needed here, a firm hand!

At the halfway point there was the large village of Rovnoye. The hot, dry wind was rushing along the empty streets and through the willows, scorched by the heat. By the doorsteps, chickens were busy covering themselves in cinders. Poking up crudely on the bare common was the weird-coloured church. Beyond the church, a shallow, clayey pond was shimmering in the sun below a dam of dung – thick, yellow water in which a herd of cows was standing, continually answering calls of nature, and a naked peasant was soaping his head. He had gone waist-deep into the water; on his chest there shone a copper cross, his neck and face were tanned black, while his trunk was astonishingly pale and white.

"Unbridle the horse, will you," said Tikhon Ilyich, driving into the pond, which smelt of the herd.

The peasant tossed a marbled, bluish piece of soap onto the bank, black with cows' droppings, and, with his head grey and soapy, covering himself modestly, he hastened to carry out the order. The horse fell upon the water greedily, but the water was so warm and unpleasant that it lifted its head and turned away. Whistling to it softly, Tikhon Ilyich shook his cap:

"What awful water you've got! Don't drink it, do you?"

"And yours is sweet as sugar, is it?" the peasant retorted, gently and cheerfully. "We've always drunk it! Who cares about the water – it's bread we haven't got…"

Beyond Rovnoye the road set off between unbroken fields of rye – again, weak and scrawny, awash with cornflowers… And near Vyselki, not far from Durnovka, a cloud of rooks with open, silvery beaks was sitting on a hollow, gnarled brittle willow – they like the sites of fires for some reason: of Vyselki in those days there remained just the name alone – just the black shells of huts amidst debris. The debris was emitting a milky-bluish smoke, there was the sour smell of ashes… And the thought of fire struck through Tikhon Ilyich like lightning. "What a calamity!" he thought, turning pale. He had nothing insured, everything could be gone in an hour…

After the fast, after that memorable journey to the fair, Tikhon Ilyich started drinking – and quite often too, not getting drunk, but getting respectably red in the face. However, this did his business no harm at all, and, in his words, did his health no harm either. "Vodka polishes the blood," he would say. Not infrequently now he would call his life a torment, a noose, a golden cage. But he strode along his path ever more surely, and several years passed so monotonously that everything merged into a single working day. And the new major events were things that had never been expected – war with Japan and revolution.

Talk of the war began, of course, with bragging. "The Cossack'll soon cut the yellowskin to ribbons, brother!" But soon different words were heard.

"We don't know what to do with our own land!" said Tikhon Ilyich in a stern, commanding tone. "This war, sir, is nothing but a nonsense!"

And he was stirred to gloating delight by news of the terrible defeats of the Russian army:

"Oh, wonderful! Let them have it, the motherfuckers!"

He was delighted at first by the Revolution too, he was delighted by the killings:

"The way he gave that minister one in the heart," Tikhon Ilyich would sometimes say in the heat of rapture, "the way he gave it him – and there was nothing left of him but dust!"

Yet as soon as they started talking about the alienation of land, the rage began to awaken within him. "It's all the Yids' work! It's all the Yids, sir, and those ragamuffins, the students, too!" And it was incomprehensible: everyone saying revolution, revolution, while all around – everything's as before, humdrum: the sun shines, the rye blooms in the fields, carts drag their way to the station... Incomprehensible in their silence, in their evasive talk, were the peasants.

"It's secretive they've become, sir, the peasants! It's just awful, how secretive!" Tikhon Ilyich would say.

And forgetting about "the Yids", he would add:

"Let's suppose this whole tune's not so devious, sir. Change the government and divide the land up equally – even a baby can understand that, sir. And so it's perfectly clear who they're supporting – the peasants, that is. But they're keeping mum, of course. And so you have to keep your eyes on them and try to *make* them keep mum. Not set them off! Otherwise, watch out: if they sense success, sense they're getting their way – they'll smash everything to smithereens, sir!"

When he read or heard that they would only be taking land away from those who had more than five hundred *desyatins*,* he himself became "a troublemaker". He even entered into arguments with the peasants. A peasant would happen to be standing by his store and saying:

"No, don't go saying that, Ilyich. At a fair valuation, then you can – take it, that is. But otherwise – no, that's not the right thing..."

It's hot, there's the smell of the pine planks piled up beside the barns opposite the yard. The hot locomotive of a goods train can be heard croaking, letting off steam behind the trees and the station buildings. Tikhon Ilyich stands hatless, narrowing his eyes and smiling slyly. He smiles and replies:

"Windbag! And if he doesn't take charge of things, but idles around?"

"Who? The master? Well, that's a different matter. There's nothing wrong with taking the whole lot away from someone like that!"

"Well that's just it!"

But different news would come – they'd be taking away less than five hundred *desyatins* too – and his soul was immediately gripped by distraction, suspicion, testiness. Everything that was done around the house began to seem repellent.

Yegorka, the assistant, was carrying flour sacks out of the store and starting to shake them out. The crown of his head wedge-like, his hair coarse and thick – "And why is it that fools have such thick hair?" – the forehead concave, the face like a lopsided egg, the eyes fishlike, goggling, and the eyelids with the white lashes of a calf seemingly stretched out onto them: it was as if there had been a shortage of skin, and if the fellow closed his eyes, he would have to let his mouth gape, and if he shut his mouth, he would need to open his eyelids wide. And Tikhon Ilyich cried angrily:

"Muddlehead! Bonehead! What are you shaking it onto me for?"

The cook was carrying out some little chest or other, opening it, putting it upside down onto the ground, and starting to bang on the bottom of it with her fist. And realizing what was going on, Tikhon Ilyich slowly shook his head:

"Oh, the housewives, God damn you! Knocking the cockroaches out, are you?"

"There's simply masses of them here!" the cook replied joyfully. "Took a look, and it's God's horrors in there!"

And grinding his teeth, Tikhon Ilyich went out onto the highway and gazed for a long time into the undulating fields in the direction of Durnovka.

His living quarters, the kitchen, the store, and the barn where the alcohol used to be on sale – it all comprised the one unit under the one iron roof. Directly abutting it on three sides were the awnings of the farmyard, which was covered with straw – and the result was a cosy square. The barns stood opposite the house, across the road. To the right was the station, to the left the highway. Beyond the highway was a small birch wood. And when Tikhon Ilyich wasn't himself, he would go out onto the highway. It ran off in a white ribbon, from one bump to the next, towards the south, dropping ever lower, along with the fields, and rising once more towards the horizon only from the distant hut where it was crossed by the railway coming from the south-east. And if one of the Durnovka peasants happened to be riding along – someone who was on the sensible, intelligent side, of course, for example Yakov, whom everyone called Yakov Mikitich because he was "rich" and mean, Tikhon Ilyich would stop him.

"You might at least buy a ruddy cap!" he cried with a grin.

Yakov, in a hat, a hempen shirt, short, sackcloth trousers and barefooted, was sitting on the edge of the cart. He pulled on the rope reins and stopped his well-fed mare.

"Hello, Tikhon Ilyich," he said in a restrained voice.

"Hello! The hat, I'm saying, it's time it was donated to the jackdaws for nesting!"

With a sly grin at the ground, Yakov nodded his head.

"It... how can I put it?... wouldn't be a bad thing. But capital, for instance, doesn't allow it."

"That's fine coming from you! We know the likes of you with your hard-luck stories! You've given your lass away, married off your lad, you've got a bit of money... What else do you want from the Lord God?"

This flattered Yakov, but made him even more reticent.

"Oh Lord!" he muttered in a tremulous voice and with a sigh. "Money... I've never had the habit of it, for instance... And the lad... what of the lad? The lad's no joy... It's got to be said straight – he's no joy!"

Like many peasants, Yakov was very touchy, and especially when it came to his family and his business. He was very secretive, but here his touchiness got the upper hand, although it was revealed only in his abrupt, tremulous speech. And to stir him up completely, Tikhon Ilyich asked sympathetically:

"No joy? Well I never! And all because of his woman?"

Looking around, Yakov scratched his chest with his fingernails:

"Because of his woman, may she be struck down and paralysed..."

"Jealous, is he?"

"Yes... She says I'm screwing her..."

And Yakov's eyes were darting about:

"She complained to her husband once, then she complained again! And that's not all – she tried to poison me! When you catch cold sometimes, for instance... you have a little smoke to ease your chest... Well, and she put a roll-up under my pillow... If I hadn't looked, I'd have been done for!"

"So what sort of a roll-up was it?"

"She'd ground up dead men's bones and put that in instead of tobacco..."

"Your lad really is a fool! He should give the bloody woman a lesson the Russian way!"

19

"No chance! It was my chest, for instance, he went for! And writhing like a snake, he was... I grab him by the head, but his hair's cut short... I grab him by his shirt front... but it's a shame to rip a shirt!"

Tikhon Ilyich shook his head, was silent for a minute, and finally resolved upon it:

"Well, and how are things over there? Are you still waiting for a revolt?"

But here the secretiveness returned to Yakov at once. He grinned and waved a hand.

"Come on!" he muttered rapidly. "What on earth do we want that for – a revolt! Our folk are peaceful... Peaceful folk..."

And he pulled on the reins as if the horse were not standing still.

"So why was there a gathering on Sunday?" Tikhon Ilyich suddenly tossed out angrily.

"A gathering? The devil knows! They made a bit of a din, for instance..."

"And I know what they were making a din about! I know!"

"Well, I'm not hiding anything... They were chattering, for instance, about a directive, like, coming out... a directive's apparently come out – on no account to work at the former price..."

It was very hurtful to think he was losing his heart for business because of some Durnovka or other. And there were only some thirty homesteads in that Durnovka. And it lay in a godforsaken ravine: a wide gully, on one side the huts, on the other the wretched little estate. And that wretched little estate was exchanging glances with the huts and waiting from day to day for some "directive"... Oh, if only he could take on a few Cossacks with whips!

But a "directive" did come out. The rumour spread one Sunday that there was a gathering in Durnovka, and a plan was being devised for an attack on the manor house. With maliciously joyful eyes, with a sensation of unusual strength and audacity, with a readiness to "break the horns of the Devil himself", Tikhon Ilyich called out: "Harness the stallion to the cabriolet," and ten minutes later he was already driving it alongside the highway towards Durnovka. The sun was setting after a rainy day into red-grey clouds, the tree trunks in the little birch wood were scarlet, the cart track, its violet-black mud standing out sharply amidst fresh greenery, was heavy. From the stallion's haunches and the breeching that shifted about on them fell pink lather. Cracking the reins firmly, Tikhon Ilyich turned off away from the railway, bore to the right by a road through the fields and, catching sight of Durnovka, began for a moment to doubt the truth of the rumours about a revolt. Peace and quiet was all around, the larks were peacefully singing their evening songs, there was the simple, calm smell of damp earth and the sweetness of wild flowers... But suddenly his gaze fell upon the fallow alongside the estate, which was densely covered with yellow melilot: the peasants' herd was grazing on the fallow! It had started, then! And jerking on the reins, Tikhon Ilyich flew past the herd, past the threshing barn, overgrown with burdock and nettles, past the low-growing cherry orchard, full of sparrows, past the stables and the servants' hut, and galloped into the yard...

And then something ugly had happened: in the twilight, frozen with anger, hurt and fear, Tikhon Ilyich sat in a field in his cabriolet. His heart was pounding, his hands were trembling, his face was burning, his hearing was as sharp as a wild animal's. He sat listening to the cries that carried from Durnovka and remembering how a crowd, which had seemed huge, had flocked, on seeing him, across the gully towards the manor house, had filled the yard with din and abuse, had bunched up by the porch and pressed him against the door. He had only had a knout in his hands. And he had brandished it, now retreating, now hurling himself desperately into the crowd. But even more freely and boldly had a stick been brandished by the advancing harness-maker – vicious, wiry, with a concave stomach, sharp-nosed, wearing boots and a purple cotton shirt. On behalf of the whole crowd he had yelled that a directive had come out to "get the thing done" – to get it done on the same day and at the same time throughout the province: to drive the itinerant farm labourers out of every estate, for locals to take over their work – at a rouble a day! And Tikhon Ilyich had yelled even more frenziedly, trying to drown the harness-maker out:

"A-ah! So that's how it is! Learnt it all from the agitators, have you, you vagabond? Got the hang of things?"

And the harness-maker had caught his words tenaciously, on the wing:

"It's you that's the vagabond!" he had howled, with the blood rushing to his face. "You, you old fool! Don't I know how much land you've got? How much, you cat-skinner? Two hundred *desyatins*? While I've got – damn it – all I've got is the size of your porch! And why? Who are

21

you? Who are you, I'm asking you? What sort of stock are you made from?"

"You remember this, Mitka!" Tikhon Ilyich had cried helplessly at last and, feeling that his head was spinning round, he hurled himself through the crowd towards his cabriolet. "Just you remember it!"

But no one had been scared by his threats – and a concerted cackling, roaring and whistling had sped in his wake... And then he had skirted around the estate, stopping in terror, listening. He had driven out onto the road, onto the crossroads, and stood with his face to the sunset, to the station, ready to strike the horse at any moment. It was very quiet, warm, damp and dark. The earth, rising towards the horizon, where a weak, reddish light was still smouldering, was as black as the abyss.

"Stand s-still, you stinker!" Tikhon Ilyich whispered through his teeth to the shifting horse. "Sti-ill!"

And from the distance there came voices and cries. And standing out from among all the voices was that of Red Vanka, who had already been sent to the Donetsk mines twice. And then above the manor house there suddenly rose a dark and fiery column: the peasants had set fire to a cabin in the garden – and a pistol forgotten in the cabin by the orchard's tenant, who had already fled back to town, had started shooting from the fire of its own accord...

It was learnt subsequently that there truly had been a miracle: on one and the same day, the peasants throughout almost the entire district had revolted. And the hotels in town were for a long time overcrowded with landowners seeking protection from the authorities. But it was with great shame that Tikhon Ilyich remembered subsequently that he had sought it too: with shame, because the entire revolt ended with the peasants making a hullabaloo throughout the district, burning and destroying a few manor houses, and then falling quiet. The harness-maker soon began appearing in the store at Vorgol again as if nothing had happened, and he took his hat off deferentially on the threshold as if not noticing that Tikhon Ilyich's face had darkened at his appearance. Rumours still circulated, however, that the men of Durnovka meant to kill Tikhon Ilyich. And he was rather scared of being out late on the road from Durnovka, and he felt in his pocket for the bulldog which made a tiresome bulge in the pocket of his wide-legged trousers, and made an oath to himself to burn Durnovka to ashes one fine night... to poison the water in the Durnovka ponds... Then the rumours ceased as well. But Tikhon Ilyich began thinking hard about getting rid of Durnovka. "It's not the money your granny has, it's the money that's in your pocket!"

That year, Tikhon Ilyich turned fifty. But the dream of becoming a father did not abandon him. And that was the cause of his encounter with Rodka.

Two years before, Rodka, a lanky, sullen fellow from Ulyanovka, had gone to work for Yakov's widower brother, Fedot; he had married, buried Fedot, who had died from over-drinking at the wedding, and had been enlisted as a soldier. And the young bride, shapely, with very white, fine skin, with a delicate flush, with eternally lowered eyelashes, had begun working at the manor house as a charwoman. And those eyelashes had got Tikhon Ilyich terribly excited. The Durnovka peasant women wear "horns" on their heads: no sooner are they married, than their plaits are laid on their crowns and covered with a headscarf to form something weird, bovine. They wear old, dark-purple, married women's skirts with braid, a white pinafore like a sarafan and bast shoes. But even in that costume Bride – that nickname stayed with her – was still good-looking. And one evening, in the dark threshing barn, where Bride was finishing the raking of the ears of grain by herself, Tikhon Ilyich, after glancing around, quickly went up to her and quickly said:

"You'll go about in ankle boots and silk shawls... I'll spare no expense!"

But Bride was silent, as if dead.

"Do you hear me?" cried Tikhon Ilyich in a whisper.

But it was as if Bride had turned to stone, with her head bent, tossing with the rake.

And so he failed to achieve anything. When suddenly Rodka appeared, sooner than expected, one-eyed. This was soon after the revolt of the Durnovka men, and Tikhon Ilyich immediately hired Rodka, along with his wife, to work at the Durnovka manor house, alluding to the fact that "you can't manage without a soldier now". Just before Ilya's Day* Rodka went off to town for new brooms and spades, while Bride was washing the floors in the house. Stepping over the puddles, Tikhon Ilyich entered the room, glanced at Bride bending down, at her white calves, splashed with dirty water, at the whole of her body, grown fuller in marriage... And suddenly he clicked the key in the lock and, somehow controlling his strength and desire particularly well, he stepped towards Bride. She straightened up quickly, lifted her excited, flushed face and, holding a wet rag in her hand, cried strangely:

"I'll give you a good whacking, my lad!"

There was the smell of hot slops, a hot body, sweat... And grabbing Bride's hand, squeezing it brutally, giving the rag a shake and knocking it free, Tikhon Ilyich caught Bride by the waist with his right arm, pressed her up against him – and in such a way that her bones cracked – and carried her into the next room, where there was a bed. And throwing her head back and widening her eyes, Bride struggled and resisted no longer...

After that it became a torment to see his own wife, to see Rodka, to know that Rodka slept with Bride and beat her savagely – day and night. And soon it became horrifying too. Inscrutable are the paths by which a jealous man reaches the truth. But Rodka reached it. Thin, one-eyed, long-armed and strong as an ape, with a small, close-cropped black head which he always kept bowed, gazing from beneath his brow with his deep-sunken, shining eye, he became terrible. As a soldier he had picked up Ukrainian words and stresses. And if Bride dared to answer back to his curt, harsh speeches, he would calmly take a leather strap, go up to her with an evil grin and ask calmly through his teeth, putting the stress on the "ing":

"Waddya sayíng?"

And he would give her such a flogging that her eyes would grow dim.

Tikhon Ilyich once stumbled upon this retribution and, unable to contain himself, cried:

"What are you doing, you swine?"

But Rodka sat down calmly on a bench and only glanced at him:

"Waddya sayíng?" he asked.

And Tikhon Ilyich hurried to slam the door...

Wild ideas now began occurring to him: to arrange things, for example, so that Rodka would be crushed somewhere by a roof or some earth... But a month passed, then another – and hope, that very hope which had intoxicated him with these ideas, deceived him cruelly: Bride had not become pregnant! Whatever was the point in continuing to play with fire after that? He needed to get rid of Rodka, throw him out, and as quickly as possible.

But who was to replace him?

Chance came to his aid. Tikhon Ilyich unexpectedly made up with his brother and persuaded him to take on the running of Durnovka.

He found out from an acquaintance in town that Kuzma had worked for a long time as a clerk for the landowner Kasatkin and, most amazing of all, had become "an author". Yes, he had apparently had a whole book of his poetry printed, and on the back it said: "available from the author".

"So-o!" drawled Tikhon Ilyich on hearing this. "That Kuzma's quite something! And what – is that what they've printed, may I ask: the work of Kuzma Krasov?"

"As is right and proper," replied the acquaintance, who was of the firm belief, however – as were many in the town – that Kuzma "filched" his poetry from books and journals.

Without stirring from the spot, there and then, at a table in Dayev's tavern Tikhon Ilyich wrote a firm and brief note to his brother: it was time for old men to be reconciled, to repent. And the reconciliation took place there too. And the next day a talk about business as well.

It was morning, the tavern was still empty. The sun was shining through the dusty windows and illuminating the tables covered with dampish red tablecloths, the dark floor, just scrubbed with grain husks and smelling of the stables, and waiters in white shirts and white trousers. A canary in a cage, as if not a real, but a clockwork one, was singing all kinds of tunes. Tikhon Ilyich sat down at a table with a nervous and serious face, and, as soon as he had ordered tea for two, the long-familiar voice rang out above his ear:

"Well, hello again."

Kuzma was shorter than him, more bony, wirier. He had a large, thin face with slightly prominent cheekbones, frowning grey brows, small greenish eyes. He began in a less than straightforward way:

"First of all I shall set out for you, Tikhon Ilyich," he began, as soon as Tikhon Ilyich had poured him some tea, "I shall set out for you who I am, so that you know..." he grinned, "who you're getting involved with..."

And he had a manner of rapping out the syllables, raising his eyebrows, undoing and doing up the top button of his jacket during conversation. And after doing himself up, he continued:

"You see, I'm an anarchist..."

Tikhon Ilyich raised his eyebrows.

"Never fear. I'm not involved in politics. But you can't stop anyone thinking. And there's no harm in it for you at all. I'll run things meticulously, but, I'm telling you straight – I won't go fleecing anyone."

"Well, the times have changed too," sighed Tikhon Ilyich.

"The times are just the same. You can still fleece people. But no, it's not fitting. I shall manage things, and I'll devote my free time to self-development... to reading, that is."

"Oh, you bear it in mind: too much reading and your pocket'll be bleeding!" said Tikhon Ilyich, tossing his head and twitching the corner of his lip. "And I reckon it's not for us."

"Well I don't think so," objected Kuzma. "I, brother – how can I explain it to you? – I'm a strange Russian type!"

"I'm a Russian myself too, bear it in mind," interjected Tikhon Ilyich.

"But different. I don't mean to say that I'm better than you, but – different. I can see that you're proud to be Russian, while I, brother, am far from being a Slavophile! It doesn't do to chatter a lot, but one thing I will say: for God's sake don't boast about being Russian. We're a savage people!"

Frowning, Tikhon Ilyich drummed his fingers on the table.

"That, I reckon, is true," he said. "A savage people. Wild."

"Well, that's exactly it. I can say I've roamed the world quite a bit – well, and? – absolutely nowhere have I seen more miserable and lazy types. And if one of them isn't lazy" – Kuzma gave his brother a sidelong look – "well, nothing good's ever come of him. He grubs around, builds himself a nest bit by bit, but what's the good of it?"

"What do you mean – what's the good of it?" asked Tikhon Ilyich.

"What I say. Building it, the nest, has to be done with purpose as well. I'll build it, like, and then I'll live like a decent person. With this and this."

And Kuzma tapped his finger on his chest and forehead.

"We've clearly got no time for that, brother," said Tikhon Ilyich. "'Come live in the village, eat grey cabbage soup, wear rotten bast shoes!'"*

"Bast shoes!" Kuzma responded caustically. "We're wearing them, brother, for the second thousand years, may they be thrice accursed. And who's to blame? The Tatars, you see, crushed us! We're a young

26

people, you see! But there too, you know, in Europe, I reckon there's been quite a bit of crushing going on as well – all sorts of Mongols. And the Germans are probably no older... Well, but that's a different conversation!"

"True!" said Tikhon Ilyich. "Better, let's talk about business."

Kuzma, however, went on with what he was saying:

"I don't go to church..."

"You're a schismatic, then?" asked Tikhon Ilyich, and thought: "I've had it! I clearly need to get rid of Durnovka!"

"A sort of schismatic," grinned Kuzma. "But do you go? If it weren't for terror and a bit of need, you'd have completely forgotten the way."

"Well, I'm not the first and I won't be the last," retorted Tikhon Ilyich, frowning. "We're all sinners. But you know, it's said: one last breath and all's forgiven."

Kuzma shook his head.

"You're saying the usual thing!" he said sternly. "But just you stop and think: how can it be? Lived and lived like a swine all his life, one breath – and everything's gone as if by magic! Is there sense in that, or not?"

The conversation was becoming difficult. "That's true as well," thought Tikhon Ilyich, gazing at the table with gleaming eyes. But, as always, he wanted to avoid thoughts and conversation about God and about life, and he said the first thing that came to his tongue:

"I'd be glad to go to heaven, but my sins won't let me."

"There you are, there you are!" Kuzma chimed in, tapping a fingernail on the table. "The thing we love best of all, our most ruinous feature: saying one thing, and doing another! A Russian tune, brother: living like a swine is bad, but I do and will live like a swine all the same! Well, talk your business then..."

The canary had grown quiet. People were gathering in the inn. Audible now from the market was the amazingly distinct and resonant warbling of a quail somewhere in a store. And while the conversation about business was going on, Kuzma kept listening to it closely, and at times he would comment in a low voice: "Canny!" And on reaching an agreement, he slapped his palm on the table and said energetically:

"Well then, so be it – no going back!" and, dipping his hand into the side pocket of his jacket, he took out a whole pile of papers, large and small, found among them a little book in a marble-grey cover, and put it down in front of his brother.

"Here you are!" he said. "I yield to your request and my own weakness. It's a wretched little book, the verse is ill-thought-out and old... But there's nothing can be done. Here, take it and put it away."

And again Tikhon Ilyich got excited that his brother was an author, that printed on this marble-grey cover was: *Poems by K.I. Krasov*. He turned the book over in his hands and said timorously:

"Or perhaps you might read something... Eh? Do be so kind and read out three or four poems!"

And lowering his head, putting on a pince-nez, holding the book out a long way away from him and gazing at it sternly through the lenses, Kuzma started to read what the self-taught usually read: imitations of Koltsov and Nikitin,* complaints against fate and need, challenges to a sinking storm cloud. But pink spots stood out on his thin cheekbones and at times his voice trembled. Tikhon Ilyich's eyes gleamed too. Whether the poetry was good or bad was unimportant – important was the fact that it had been composed by his own brother, a poor man, an ordinary man, who smelt of cheap tobacco and old boots...

"Well we, Kuzma Ilyich," he said, when Kuzma had fallen silent and, taking off the pince-nez, had cast his eyes down, "well we have just the one song..."

And he twitched his lip unpleasantly, bitterly:

"We have just the one song: what costs what?"

Having installed his brother at Durnovka, however, he set about that song even more willingly than ever. Before passing Durnovka into his brother's hands, he found fault with Rodka over some new tugs that were eaten by the dogs, and dismissed him. Rodka grinned insolently in reply and went calmly to his hut to gather his belongings. Bride seemed to hear out the dismissal calmly too – after breaking with Tikhon Ilyich, she had again adopted a manner of remaining impassively silent, of not looking him in the eye. But half an hour later, when they were already set to go, Rodka came with her to beg forgiveness. Bride stood on the threshold, pale, her eyelids swollen with tears, silent; Rodka bowed his head, crumpled his cap and tried to cry as well, pulling repellent faces, while Tikhon Ilyich sat and contorted his eyebrows, clicking on the abacus. He was merciful only in one respect – he did not make a deduction for the tugs.

Now he was firm. While ridding himself of Rodka and handing business over to his brother, he felt cheerful, fine. "He's unreliable, my

28

brother, a shallow man, it would seem, but he'll do for the moment!"
And on returning to Vorgol, he was tirelessly busy for the whole of
October. And, as if in harmony with his mood, for the whole of
October the weather was wonderful. But suddenly it broke, and was
followed by a storm, torrential rains, and in Durnovka something
entirely unexpected happened.

Rodka was working on the railway line in October, while Bride stayed
at home with nothing to do, just occasionally earning fifteen or twenty
kopeks in the orchard on the estate. She behaved strangely: at home she
was silent and cried, but in the orchard she was abruptly cheerful, she
laughed loudly, and sang songs with Donka Nanny-goat, a very silly
and pretty lass who looked like an Egyptian. Nanny-goat lived with
the man from town who was renting the orchard, and Bride, who had
made friends with her for some reason, threw provocative looks at his
brother, an impudent boy, and as she threw them, she hinted in her songs
that she was pining for someone. Whether there was anything between
them is unknown, only it all ended in great misfortune: leaving for
town on the eve of the Virgin of Kazan's Day,* the townsmen organized
"a little party" in their cabin – they invited Nanny-goat and Bride,
played two squeeze boxes all night, gave the girls a pawing and tea
and vodka to drink, and at dawn, when they were already harnessing
the cart, suddenly, with loud laughter, they tumbled the drunken Bride
to the ground, tied her arms together, lifted her skirts, gathered them
into a plait above her head and twisted a rope around them. Nanny-
goat ran away, in terror took refuge in the tall, wet weeds, and when
she peeped out of them – after the cart with the townsmen had rolled
swiftly away out of the orchard – she saw that Bride, bare below the
waist, was hanging from a tree. It was a mournful, misty dawn, a light
rain was whispering through the orchard, Nanny-goat cried floods of
tears and her teeth chattered as she untied Bride, and she swore on the
lives of her father and mother that she, Nanny-goat, would be struck by
a thunderbolt before they found out in the village what had happened
in the orchard... But not even a week had gone by before rumours of
Bride's disgrace began spreading through Durnovka.

It was, of course, impossible to verify those rumours: "no one had
seen anything, well, and it wouldn't take much to make Nanny-goat
lie." The gossip provoked by the rumours did not cease, however, and
everyone awaited with great impatience the arrival of Rodka and his

punishment of his wife. An agitated Tikhon Ilyich – knocked out of his stride again! – awaited this punishment too, having learnt of the episode in the orchard from his workmen: after all, the episode might end in murder! But it ended in such a way that it is still uncertain what would have shocked Durnovka more – a murder or an end such as that: the night before St Michael's Day,* Rodka, who had come home "to change his shirt", died "because of his stomach"! This became known in Vorgol late in the evening, but Tikhon Ilyich immediately ordered a horse to be harnessed, and in the darkness, in the rain, he rushed off to see his brother. And in the heat of the moment, having drunk a bottle of fruit liqueur over tea, in passionate expressions and with darting eyes, he confessed to him:

"It's my fault, brother, it's my fault!"

After hearing him out, Kuzma was silent for a long time, for a long time he walked around the room, playing with his fingers, wringing them and cracking the joints. Finally, out of the blue he said:

"Just you think now: is there any people crueller than ours? In town, a petty thief who's grabbed the cheapest flat cake from a tray is chased by folk from the entire row of refreshment stalls, and when they catch him they make him eat soap. The whole town runs to see a fire or a fight, and how sorry they are that the fire or the fight is soon over! Don't shake your head, don't, they are sorry! And how people enjoy it when someone's beating his wife to death, or beating a boy black and blue, or making fun of him! Now that really is the jolliest thing that can be."

"Bear it in mind," Tikhon Ilyich interrupted him hotly, "there've always been a lot of sneering people everywhere."

"Right. And haven't you yourself had that… well, what's his name? That simpleton?"

"Motya Duckhead, do you mean?" asked Tikhon Ilyich.

"Yes, that's it, that's it… Haven't you had him brought to your place for amusement?"

And Tikhon Ilyich grinned: he had. Motya had even been delivered to him once by rail – in a sugar barrel. He knew the railway officials – well, and he'd been delivered. And they'd written on the barrel: "With care. Complete idiot."

"And for amusement they teach these simpletons to masturbate!" Kuzma continued bitterly. "They daub tar on poor unmarried women's gates! They set dogs on beggars! They knock doves off roofs with stones for fun! But to eat those doves is a great sin, don't you know. The Holy Ghost Himself, don't you know, takes the form of a dove!"

The samovar had grown cold long before, the candle had guttered, the smoke in the room was a dull blue, the entire slop basin was full of stinking, sodden cigarette butts. The ventilator – a tin pipe in the top corner of a window – was open, and something inside it would at times begin to shriek, spin round and moan ever so drearily – "like in the parish council," thought Tikhon Ilyich. But there was so much cigarette smoke that even ten ventilators would not have helped. And the rain was making a noise on the roof, and Kuzma was going from corner to corner like a pendulum and saying:

"Ye-es, we're nice ones, indeed we are! Indescribable goodness! If you read some history, your hair'll stand on end: brother against brother, in-law against in-law, son against father, treachery and killing, killing and treachery... the old Russian epics are nothing but pleasure too: 'ripped his white breast open', 'spilt his guts out onto the ground'... Ilya, well he 'stepped on the left foot' of his own daughter and 'pulled on the right foot'... And the songs? It's all the same, all the same: the stepmother's 'evil and grasping', a bride's father-in-law's 'fierce and carping', 'he sits on the stove bench like a dog on a rope', the mother-in-law, again, is 'fierce', 'she sits on the stove like a bitch on a chain', sisters-in-law are sure to be 'little bitches and telltales', the brothers-in-law are 'vicious scoffers', the husband is 'either a fool or a drunkard', his father, the father-in-law, bids him 'beat his wife hard, give her a good thrashing', while for that same father the nice little daughter-in-law has 'washed the floor, and poured it into his soup, scrubbed the doorstep, and put it into his pie', and she addresses her dear husband with words such as these: 'get up, you hateful man, awake; here, take the slops and wash yourself; here, take your puttees and wipe yourself; here, take a bit of rope and hang yourself'... And our funny sayings, Tikhon Ilyich! Can anything filthier and smuttier be invented? And the proverbs! 'For one beaten man you get two unbeaten'... 'Simplicity is worse than thievery'..."

"So according to you, is it better to live like a beggar?" asked Tikhon Ilyich mockingly.

And Kuzma picked up joyfully on his words:

"There now, there! There's none in all the world more destitute than us, but at the same time there's none more sneering about that same

31

destitution. How do you wound a man really viciously? With poverty! 'Damn it! You've got no grub…' Here's an example for you: Deniska… you know the one… Grey's son… the cobbler… he says to me the other day—"

"Hang on," Tikhon Ilyich interrupted, "and how's Grey himself?"

"Deniska says: 'he's dying of hunger'."

"The man's a stinker!" said Tikhon Ilyich with conviction. "Don't you sing me any songs about him."

"I'm not going to," replied Kuzma angrily. "Better, listen about Deniska. Here's what he tells me: 'In a hungry year we used to go out, the apprentices, to the Chornaya Sloboda, and there were these prostitoots there, loads of them. And hungry, the greedy cows, really hungry! Give her half a pound of bread for all her work, and she'd pig down the lot of it underneath you… What a laugh it was!…' After all that!" cried Kuzma sternly, stopping. "'What a laugh it was!'"

"Just hang on, for Christ's sake," Tikhon Ilyich interrupted again, "let me say a word about that other business!"

Kuzma stopped.

"Well, go on," he said. "Only what is there to say? What are you to do? Nothing! Give her some money – and that's all there is to it. Just think of it, after all: nothing for heating, nothing to eat, no money for the funeral! And then take her on again. To cook for me…"

Tikhon Ilyich left for home at first light on a cold, misty morning, while there was still the smell of wet threshing floors and smoke, the cockerels were still singing sleepily in the village, hidden by the mist, the dogs were asleep by the porch, and so was the old, straw-coloured turkey, which had clambered up onto a bough of a half-bare apple tree, coloured with dead autumn leaves, beside the house. In the fields, nothing was visible two paces away in the dense, grey haze that was driven on by the wind. Tikhon Ilyich was not sleepy, but he did feel exhausted and, as always, drove his horse hard – a big bay mare with its tail tied up, which, sodden, seemed thinner, more dandified, blacker. He turned away from the wind, raised the right side of the cold, damp collar of his *chuika*, which was silvery from the tiniest beads of rain that completely covered it, and he gazed through the cold little drops hanging on his eyelashes at the way the sticky black earth gathered ever more thickly on his speeding wheel, at the way there hung unceasingly before him a whole fountain of high-pounding clods of mud, which was already clinging everywhere onto his boots and knees, and he looked sidelong at the working haunch of the horse, at its flattened ears, indistinct in the mist... And when he at last flew up to the house, his face speckled with mud, the first thing that struck him was Yakov's horse at the tethering post. Quickly winding the reins around the front of the cabriolet, he leapt down from it, ran up to the open door of the store – and stopped in fright.

"Windba-ag!" Nastasya Petrovna was saying behind the counter, evidently imitating him, Tikhon Ilyich, but in a sick, affectionate voice, and bending ever lower towards the chest of money, rummaging in the jangling copper, but unable to find in the darkness the coin to give as change. "Windbag! Where is it cheaper nowadays?"

And without finding the coin, she unbent herself, looked at Yakov standing in front of her in a hat and *armyak*,* but barefooted, at his crooked beard of indeterminate colour, and added:

"Did she maybe poison him?"

And Yakov muttered hastily:

"That's no business of ours, Petrovna... The devil knows... Our business is to keep out of it... To keep out of it, for instance..."

And Tikhon Ilyich's hands were trembling all day at the memory of that muttering. They all think she poisoned him, all of them!

Fortunately, the mystery remained just that, a mystery: Rodka was buried, Bride keened so sincerely as she accompanied the coffin, it was even unseemly – after all, the keening wasn't supposed to be an expression of feelings, but the execution of a rite – and little by little Tikhon Ilyich's alarm subsided.

Besides, he was up to his neck in work, yet had no helping hands. Nastasya Petrovna was of little help. Tikhon Ilyich only hired seasonal workers as farm labour until the autumn feast days. And they had already left. There remained only the annual workers – the cook, the old watchman nicknamed Seedcake, and the lad Oska, "an absolute imbecile". And the amount of care demanded by the livestock alone! There were twenty sheep overwintering. Sitting in the sty there were six black boars, eternally sullen and discontented about something. In the farmyard stood three cows, a steer and a red calf. In the backyard there were eleven horses, and in the stalls the grey stallion, bad-tempered, heavy, full-maned, deep-chested – a lout, but four hundred roubles' worth: its father had had a pedigree and cost fifteen hundred. And it all demanded eyes and yet more eyes.

Nastasya Petrovna had long been planning to go and stay with acquaintances in town. And she did finally make her mind up and leave. After seeing her off, Tikhon Ilyich wandered aimlessly into the fields. Walking along the highway with a gun over his shoulders was the head of the post office in Ulyanovka, Sakharov, well-known for such a ferocious attitude to the peasants that they said: "When you give him a letter, your hands and legs are shaking!" Tikhon Ilyich went over to the side of the road to him. Raising an eyebrow, he glanced at him and thought:

"Stupid old man. Look at him, splashing his boots through the mud."

And he called out amicably:

"Good hunting, was it, Anton Markych?"

The postman stopped. Tikhon Ilyich went over and said hello.

"Come on now, what hunting!" was the gloomy reply of the postman, huge, stooping, with thick grey hair sticking out of his ears and nostrils, big, arching eyebrows and deeply sunken eyes. "I've just been out for a stroll for the good of my haemorrhoids," he said, making a particular effort with the pronunciation of the last word.

"Well bear it in mind," responded Tikhon Ilyich with unexpected fervour, reaching out a hand with the fingers spread wide, "bear it in mind: our homelands are completely empty now! Nothing left, not even the name, sir, be it bird or beast!"

"The woods have been cut down everywhere," said the postman.

"And how, sir! How they've been cut down, sir! Down to the ground!" Tikhon Ilyich chimed in.

And added unexpectedly:

"Shedding, sir! Everything's shedding, sir!"

Why that word escaped his lips, Tikhon Ilyich himself was unaware, but he felt that it had not been said without reason all the same. "Everything's shedding," he thought, "yes, like the livestock after a long and difficult winter..." And after saying goodbye to the postman, he stood for a long time on the highway, looking around discontentedly. It was beginning to drizzle again, there was an unpleasant, damp wind. Above the undulating fields – winter fields, ploughed fields, stubble fields, brown copses – it was getting dark. The gloomy sky was descending ever lower towards the earth. The rain-flooded roads gleamed like tin. People were waiting for the post train to Moscow at the station, and from there came the smell of the samovar, arousing a melancholy desire for comfort, a warm, clean room, a family or a departure for somewhere...

It poured with rain again in the night, and the darkness was black as pitch. Tikhon Ilyich slept badly, ground his teeth agonizingly. He felt shivery – he'd probably caught a cold, standing on the highway in the evening – the *chuika* with which he had covered himself was slipping off onto the floor, and then he dreamt of what had haunted him ever since childhood, when his back had grown cold in the night: twilight, some narrow side streets, a running crowd, firemen galloping on heavy carts, on bad-tempered black carthorses... Once he awoke, lit a match, glanced at the alarm clock – it showed three – picked up the *chuika* and, falling asleep again, began to feel alarmed: they'd rob the store, steal the horses...

Sometimes it seemed to him that he was at the inn in Dankov, that the rain in the night was making a noise on the roof over the gates, and the bell above them was continually jerking, ringing – thieves had come, they had brought his stallion into this impenetrable darkness, and if they found out he was here, they would kill him... And sometimes his consciousness of reality would return. Yet reality was alarming too. The old man was walking about with his rattle outside the windows, yet one moment he would seem to be somewhere far, far away, and the next Buyan would be tearing at somebody frenziedly, running off into the fields and barking wildly, but then suddenly turning up outside the windows again, waking him up by standing on the spot and yelping persistently. At that point Tikhon Ilyich would mean to go out and see what was the matter, whether everything was all right. But as soon as it came to making up his mind and getting up, the heavy, slanting rain would begin rattling thicker and faster against the dark little windows, driven by the wind from the dark, boundless fields, and sleep seemed dearer than father and mother...

Finally the door banged, there was a waft of damp cold – and Seedcake the watchman, making a rustling noise, dragged a truss of straw into the hall. Tikhon Ilyich opened his eyes: there was a turbid, watery dawn, the little windows were misted over.

"Heat the place up, brother, heat it up," said Tikhon Ilyich in a voice husky from sleep. "And we'll go and feed the animals, then you can go and get some sleep."

The old man, grown thinner in the course of the night and completely blue with the cold, damp and tiredness, glanced at him with his sunken, dead eyes. In a wet hat, in a wet *chekmen** and tattered bast shoes, soaked with water and mud, he started growling something in a muffled voice, kneeling down with difficulty in front of the stove, filling it with cold, strong-smelling haulm and lighting a sulphur spill.

"What, has the cow chewed your tongue off?" cried Tikhon Ilyich huskily, climbing down from his bed. "What are you muttering under your breath about?"

"After roaming around the entire night, now it's feed the animals," the old man mumbled, without raising his head, as though to himself.

Tikhon Ilyich looked askance at him:

"I saw the way you were roaming around!"

He put on his *poddyovka* and, overcoming the slight tremor in his stomach, he went out onto the well-trampled little porch, into the icy freshness of the pale, inclement morning. There were leaden puddles everywhere, all the walls were dark with rain...

"Bloody workmen!" he thought bad-temperedly.

It was barely drizzling, "but it'll probably be pouring down again by lunchtime," he thought. And he glanced with surprise at shaggy Buyan, who had hurtled towards him from around a corner: eyes shining, tongue fresh and red as fire, hot breath simply ablaze with the smell of dog... And this after a whole night of running around and barking!

He took Buyan by the collar and, splashing through the mud, he went round and examined all the locks. Then he put him on a chain by the granary, returned to the lobby and glanced into the large kitchen, into the hut. There was an unpleasant, warm stench in the hut; the cook was asleep on a bare bench with her apron over her face, her rump sticking out, and her legs bent up towards her stomach in their big, old, felt boots, their soles thick with dirt from the earthen floor; Oska lay on the plank bed in a knee-length sheepskin coat and bast shoes with his head buried in a greasy, heavy pillow.

"It's like stealing from a baby!" thought Tikhon Ilyich with disgust. "Look at her, debauchery all night long, and with morning coming – she's out on the bench!"

And after casting an eye over the black walls, the tiny little windows, the tub of slops and the huge, broad-shouldered stove, he cried out loudly and sternly:

"Hey! Gentlemen boyars! Time's up!"

While the cook was lighting the stove, boiling potatoes for the boars and blowing the samovar into life, Oska, hatless and stumbling from sleepiness, lugged chaff to the horses and cows. Tikhon Ilyich opened up the creaking gates of the farmyard himself and was the first into its warm and muddy cosiness, enclosed by awnings, loose boxes and pigsties. The farmyard was strewn with dung above ankle height. Dung, urine, rain – it had all blended to form a thick, brown slush. The horses, already darkening with their velvety winter coats, wandered about under the awnings. The sheep had bunched together into one corner in a dirty grey mass. The old brown gelding was drowsing alone beside the empty manger, all smeared with viscous matter. From the bleak, inclement sky above the square of the yard it drizzled and drizzled. The boars moaned painfully, insistently, and rumbled in the pigsty.

"Dismal!" thought Tikhon Ilyich, and immediately barked ferociously at the old man dragging a truss of haulm:

"Why on earth are you dragging it through the dirt, you old blatherer?"

The old man threw the haulm onto the ground, gave him a look and suddenly said calmly:

"You're a blatherer yourself."

Tikhon Ilyich looked around quickly to see if the boy had come out, and, satisfied that he had, he quickly and also seemingly calmly went up to the old man, gave him one in the teeth, enough to make him shake his head, then grabbed him by the scruff of the neck and flung him with all his strength towards the gates.

"Out!" he cried, choking and turning white as chalk. "And never let me set eyes on you round here again, you scum!"

The old man flew out of the gates – and five minutes later, with a sack over his shoulders and with a stick in his hand, he was already striding home along the highway. With shaking hands, Tikhon Ilyich watered the stallion, poured some fresh oats out for it – those of the day before it had only dug over and slobbered on – and with broad strides, sinking in the slush and the dung, he went off to the hut.

"Ready, is it?" he cried, opening the door a little.

"What's the hurry!" snapped the cook.

The hut was clouded with the warm, flavourless steam from the potatoes, which was pouring out of a cast-iron pot. The cook and the boy were together pounding them furiously with pestles, sprinkling them with flour, and Tikhon Ilyich could not hear the reply above the banging. Slamming the door, he went to have tea.

In the small hall he kicked the dirty, heavy mat lying by the doorstep and headed into the corner, where a copper water dispenser was fixed above a tin basin on a stool, and on a shelf lay a little soiled cake of coconut soap. Making a clatter with the water dispenser, he squinted, shifted his eyebrows, flared his nostrils, unable to stop his angry, darting glance, and with particular clarity said:

"Hmm! No, what about those workmen, sir! They've got right out of hand nowadays! You say one word to him, and he answers you back with ten! Say ten to him, and he answers you back with a hundred! No, you're talking rubbish! I reckon it's not the summer coming, and I reckon there's a lot of you about, you devils. It's the winter, brother, and you'll be wanting to eat – and you'll be here, you son of a bitch, you'll be he-ere, bowing do-own!"

The hand towel had been hanging beside the water dispenser since St Michael's Day. It was so dirty that, glancing at it, Tikhon Ilyich clenched his jaws.

"Oh!" he said, closing his eyes and shaking his head. "Oh, Mother, Queen of Heaven!"

Two doors led from the hall. One, to the left, into the guest room, long, in semi-darkness, with little windows facing the farmyard; in it stood two large divans, hard as rock, upholstered in black oilcloth, and full of bedbugs, both live and squashed, dried-up ones, while on the pier there hung a portrait of a general with dashing, beaverish sideburns; the portrait was fringed with smaller portraits of heroes of the Russo-Turkish War, and at the bottom was the inscription: "Long will our children and our Slavic brothers remember the glorious deeds, when our father, the bold warrior, beat Suleiman Pasha, defeated the infidel enemy and with his children crossed places so steep that only the mists and the lords of the feathered world flew there." The other door led into the room of the master and mistress. There, on the right, beside the door, shone the glass panes of a cabinet, and on the left was the whiteness of a stove and stove bench; the stove had cracked at some point, and the crack had been filled, over the white, with clay – and the result had been the outlines of something resembling a twisted, thin man, of whom Tikhon Ilyich was well and truly sick. Behind the stove there towered a double bed; fixed up above the bed was a rug of dull-green and brick-red wool with the image of a tiger, whiskered and with protruding feline ears. Opposite the door, by the wall, stood a chest of drawers, covered with a knitted tablecloth, and on it was Nastasya Petrovna's wedding casket...

"You're wanted in the store!" cried the cook, opening the door a little.

The far distance was hidden in a watery mist, it was beginning to look like dusk again, there was drizzling rain, but the wind had turned and was blowing from the north – and the air had freshened. More cheerful and resonant than in all recent days was the cry of a departing goods train at the station.

With a nod of his wet Manchurian fur hat, a harelipped peasant standing by the porch holding a wet, skewbald horse said: "Hello, Ilyich."

"Hello," Tikhon Ilyich tossed out, looking askance at the strong, white tooth shining from behind the peasant's split lip. "What do you want?"

And after hurriedly serving him with salt and paraffin, he hurriedly returned to his living quarters.

"They don't give me time to cross myself, the dogs!" he muttered as he went.

The samovar standing on the table beside the pier was seething and gurgling, and the little mirror hanging above the table had a coating of white steam. Moisture cloaked the windows and the oleograph nailed below the mirror – a giant in a yellow kaftan and red morocco boots with the Russian banner in his hands, from behind which looked the towers and cupolas of the Moscow Kremlin. Photographs in tortoiseshell frames surrounded this picture. In the place of honour hung a portrait of a renowned priest in a moiré cassock, with a straggly little beard, slightly swollen cheeks and piercing little eyes. And after glancing at it, Tikhon Ilyich crossed himself devoutly before the icon in the corner. Then he took the smoke-blackened teapot from the samovar and poured a glass of tea, which smelt strongly of steamed birch twigs.

"They don't give me time to cross myself," he thought, with a frown of suffering. "They've done for me, curse them!"

He seemed to need to remember something, to grasp something or simply to lie down and have a proper sleep. He wanted warmth, peace, clarity, firmness of thought. He got up, went over to the cabinet, making its panes of glass and the crockery tinkle, and took from a shelf a bottle of rowan-berry vodka and a stocky little glass, on which was written: "even the monks take it"...

"Or perhaps I shouldn't?" he said out loud.

But he poured some out and drank it, poured again and drank again. And having a thick pretzel to eat with the drink, he sat down at the table.

He gulped hot tea greedily from a saucer and sucked on a lump of sugar, holding it on his tongue. While gulping down the tea, he threw an absent-minded and suspicious sidelong glance at the pier, at the peasant in the yellow kaftan, at the photographs in the tortoiseshell frames, and even at the priest in the moiré cassock.

"We pigs have got no time for lerigion!" he thought, and, as if justifying himself to somebody, added rudely: "Come live in the village, eat sour cabbage soup!"

Looking sidelong at the priest, he felt that everything was dubious... even, it seemed, his usual reverence towards this priest... dubious and not thought through. If you gave it a bit of thought... But here he hastened to transfer his gaze to the Moscow Kremlin.

"It's a distgrace to admit it!" he muttered. "But I've never been to Moscow!"

No, he never had. And why? The boars forbade it! First the trading didn't let him, then the inn, then the tavern. And now it was the stallion and the boars that didn't let him. Moscow – that was nothing! He'd spent ten years meaning in vain to go to the little birch wood that was over the highway. He was forever hoping to snatch a free evening somehow, take a rug with him, the samovar, and sit on the grass in the cool, in the greenery – and he never had snatched one... The days slip by like water through your fingers, and before you'd had time to realize it – you'd hit fifty, and it'd soon be the end of everything, yet was it really so long ago he was running around with no trousers on? It seemed like yesterday!

The faces watched motionless from the tortoiseshell frames. There on the ground (but amidst dense rye) lie two people – Tikhon Ilyich himself and a young merchant, Rostovtsev – holding glasses in their hands, exactly half full of dark beer... What a friendship was to be struck up between Rostovtsev and Tikhon Ilyich! How he remembered that grey day at Shrovetide when they had been photographed! But what year had it been? Where had Rostovtsev disappeared to? You couldn't be certain now whether he had even been alive or not... And there, standing up straight to attention and turned to stone, are three townsmen, their hair combed flat with a straight parting, in embroidered *kosovorotkas*, long frock coats, shiny boots – Buchnev, Vystavkin and Bogomolov. In front of his chest, Vystavkin, the one in the middle, is holding bread and salt on a wooden platter, covered with a towel embroidered with cockerels, Buchnev and Bogomolov are each holding an icon. These were photographed on the dusty, windy day when the elevator was blessed – when the Bishop and the Governor had come, when Tikhon Ilyich had felt so proud of the fact that he had been among the members of the public who had greeted the authorities. But what remained of that day in his memory? Only the fact that they had waited about five hours beside the elevator, that a cloud of white dust had flown on the wind, that the Governor, a tall and clean corpse of a man in white trousers with gold stripes, in a gold-embroidered tunic and cocked hat, had walked towards the deputation extraordinarily slowly... that it had been really frightening when he had started speaking, accepting the bread and salt, and that everyone had been struck by the extraordinary thinness and whiteness of his hands and by their skin, the most delicate and shiny, like the skin stripped from a snake, and by the shining rings, some with cloudy stones, on his wiry, slender fingers with long, transparent nails... That Governor was no longer alive now, and Vystavkin was no longer alive either... And in five or ten years they would be saying the same of Tikhon Ilyich as well:

"The late Tikhon Ilyich..."

The room was warmer and cosier thanks to the stove's heating up, the little mirror had cleared, but outside the windows nothing was to be seen, the panes were white with matt steam, meaning that outside it was getting fresher. Ever more audibly came the tedious groaning of the hungry boars – and suddenly that groaning turned into a friendly and powerful roar: the boars had doubtless heard the voices of the cook and Oska, as they lugged a heavy tub of mash towards them. And without finishing his thoughts about death, Tikhon Ilyich threw his cigarette into the slop basin, pulled on his *poddyovka* and hastened to the farmyard. Taking broad and deep strides through the squelching dung, he himself opened the pigsty – and for a long time he kept his greedy and mournful eyes fixed on the boars, who had rushed to the trough into which the steaming mash had been poured.

The thought about death was interrupted by another: deceased he might be, but perhaps this deceased man would be cited as an example. Who was he? An orphan, a beggar, who hadn't eaten a piece of bread for two days at a time as a child... And now?

"Your life story ought to be described," Kuzma had said in mockery one day.

But there was really nothing to mock. It meant he had his head on his shoulders, if a beggarly little boy who could barely read had become not Tishka, but Tikhon Ilyich.*

Suddenly the cook, who was also gazing intently at the boars as they jostled one another and dropped their front legs into the trough, gave a hiccup and said:

"Oh Lord! I hope there'll be no misfortune today! I had this dream last night – it was as if we'd had livestock driven into the yard, all sorts of sheep, cows, pigs... And they were all black, all black!"

And again something began gnawing at his heart. Yes, that there livestock! The livestock alone was enough to make you hang yourself. Not three hours had passed – again pick up the keys, again lug fodder to the whole of the yard. In the shared loose box there are the three milk cows, in separate ones – the red calf and the bull, Bismarck: they had to be given hay now. The horses and sheep are supposed to have haulm at lunchtime, and the stallion – the Devil himself couldn't imagine what! The stallion poked his head through the barred upper part of the door, raised its top lip, bared its pink gums and white teeth, distorted its nostrils... And Tikhon Ilyich, with a fury that was unexpected even for him, suddenly shouted at it:

"Stop it, you cursed animal, may you be struck down!"

Again he got his feet wet and got cold – it was sleeting – and again he drank some rowan-berry vodka. He ate some potatoes with sunflower oil and gherkins, cabbage soup with mushrooms, millet porridge... His face flushed red, his head grew heavy.

Without undressing – only using his feet to pull off his dirty boots – he lay down on the bed. But he was troubled by the fact that he would soon have to get up again: the horses, cows and sheep need to be given oat straw towards evening, the stallion too... or no, better mix it up with hay, and then give it a good sprinkling of water and salt... Only you're sure to oversleep, aren't you, if you give yourself free rein. And Tikhon Ilyich reached out towards the chest of drawers, picked up the alarm clock and started winding it. And the alarm clock came to life, began ticking – and the room seemed to become more peaceful to the sound of its rhythmic, measured tick. His thoughts became blurred...

But no sooner had they become blurred than all of a sudden some coarse and loud church singing rang out. Opening his eyes in fright, Tikhon Ilyich could at first make out only one thing: two peasants were yelling through their noses, and there was cold and the smell of wet *chekmens* coming from the hall. Then he gave a start, sat up and looked to see who they were: one was a blind man, pockmarked, with a small nose, a long upper lip and a large, round skull, while the other was Makar Ivanovich himself!

Makar Ivanovich had once been simply Makarka – that was what everyone had called him: "Makarka the Wanderer" – and one day he had dropped into Tikhon Ilyich's tavern. He had been plodding along the highway to somewhere or other – in bast shoes, a skullcap and a greasy cassock – and in he had dropped. In his hands had been a tall staff coated with verdigris, with a cross at the top end and a sharp metal point at the bottom, over his shoulders were a satchel and a soldier's water bottle; his hair was long and yellow; his face was wide, the colour of putty, his nostrils were like two gun muzzles, his nose was broken into the shape of a wooden saddle frame, and his eyes, as is often the case with such noses, were light and sharply shining. Shameless, quick on the uptake, greedily smoking cigarette after cigarette and letting the smoke out through his nostrils, speaking rudely and curtly in a tone that completely ruled out disagreement, he had very much taken Tikhon Ilyich's fancy, and precisely for that tone – for the fact that it was clear at once: "a double-dyed son of a bitch".

And Tikhon Ilyich had taken him on – as his assistant. Got rid of his vagrant's clothing and taken him on. But Makarka had proved to be such a thief that he had been obliged to give him a cruel beating and throw him out. A year later, though, Makarka had become famous throughout the district for his prophecies, which were ominous to such a degree that people began to fear his visits like fire. He would go up to somebody's window and dolefully strike up "Repose with the saints", or he would proffer a little bit of incense or a pinch of dust, and then someone in the house would be bound to die.

And now, in his former clothing and with the staff in his hand, Makarka was standing by the threshold singing. The blind man would join in, rolling his milky eyes up towards his forehead, and from the incongruity of his features Tikhon Ilyich immediately had him down as a runaway convict, a terrible and merciless beast. But even more terrible was what these vagrants were singing. The blind man, gloomily shifting his raised eyebrows, would break out boldly in a loathsome nasal tenor. Makarka, his immobile eyes flashing sharply, droned in a ferocious bass. The result was something immoderately loud, crudely harmonious, Old Churchly, powerful and menacing:

Mother Earth will burst into tears, burst out in sobs!

the blind man poured out.

Burst in-to tears, burst out in sobs!

Makarka sang the second part with conviction.

Before the Saviour, before the icon,

the blind man wailed.

Sinners they must then repent!

Makarka threatened, opening his insolent nostrils wide. And mingling his bass with the blind man's tenor, he articulated firmly:

They shall not escape the judgement of God!
They shall not escape the fire eternal!

And suddenly he broke off – in concert with the blind man – wheezed, and simply, in his normal, insolent tone, ordered:
"Give us a little glass to get warm, merchant."

And without waiting for a reply, he stepped over the threshold, came up to the bed and shoved some sort of picture into Tikhon Ilyich's hand.

It was an ordinary cutting from an illustrated journal, but, having glanced at it, Tikhon Ilyich felt a sudden coldness in the pit of his stomach. Beneath the picture, which depicted trees bending in a storm, a white zigzag over clouds and a falling man, was the inscription: "Jean-Paul Richter, killed by lightning".*

And Tikhon Ilyich was taken aback.

But he slowly tore the picture into tiny shreds at once. Then he climbed off the bed and, pulling on his boots, said:

"Go and frighten someone stupider than me. I know you well, brother! Have what's due to you, and may God go with you."

Then he went into the store, brought two pounds of pretzels and a couple of salted herrings out to Makarka, who was standing with the blind man beside the porch, and repeated even more sternly:

"May the Lord go with you!"

"What about some tobacco?" asked Makarka insolently.

"I've only got a bit for myself," snapped Tikhon Ilyich. "Don't think you can argue with me, brother!"

And, after a pause, he added:

"Hanging's too good for you, Makarka, for your tricks!"

Makarka looked at the blind man standing upright and steady with his eyebrows raised high, and asked him:

"Man of God, what do you think? Hanging or shooting?"

"Shooting's more reliable," replied the blind man seriously. "There's a derect connection at least."

Dusk was falling, ridges of unbroken cloud were turning blue, growing cold, breathing winter. The mud was hardening. Having sent Makarka on his way, Tikhon Ilyich stamped his frozen feet on the porch for a while and went into his room. There, without taking his things off, he sat down on a chair by the window, lit a cigarette and fell into thought. He remembered the summer, the revolt, Bride, his brother, his wife... and the fact that he had still not paid the monies due for the seasonal work. It was his way to drag out payments. Lads and lasses who came to him to do day labour stood at his door for days on end in the autumn, they complained of the most extreme need, became irritable and were sometimes

45

rude. But he was unbending. He would shout, calling upon God as his witness, that he had "in all the house but two kopeks – search it, if you like!", he would turn out his pockets and his purse, spit in feigned rage, as if stunned by the mistrust, "the brazenness" of the petitioners... And now this seemed to him not to be a good way. He was mercilessly strict and cold with his wife, uncommonly aloof with her. And suddenly this too stunned him: my God, I mean, he didn't even have any conception what sort of person she was! How had she lived, what had she thought, what had she felt all these long years she had lived with him in incessant worry?

He threw the cigarette away and lit another... Oh, he's a clever one, that rogue Makarka! And since he's such a clever one, can't he foretell what's in store for whom and when? For him, Tikhon Ilyich, there was bound to be something nasty in store. He was no longer young, after all! How many of his contemporaries had already passed on! And there was no salvation from death and old age. Children wouldn't have saved him either. He wouldn't have known his children either, and he'd have been a stranger to his children, as he was to all his nearest and dearest – both living and dead. People on earth are like the stars in the sky; but life is so short, people grow up, reach manhood and die so quickly, they know each other so little and forget all they've lived through so quickly, that you'll go mad if you think about it properly! Just now he'd said of himself:

"My life ought to be described..."

But what was there to describe? Nothing. Nothing, or nothing worthwhile. After all, he himself remembered almost nothing of that life. He'd completely forgotten his childhood, for example: just from time to time some summer's day would come to him, some episode, some contemporary... He'd singed someone's cat one day – and been thrashed. He'd been given a little whip and a tin whistle – and been made indescribably happy. His drunken father had called him over to him once – affectionately, with sadness in his voice:

"Come to me, Tisha, come, my dear!"

And had unexpectedly grabbed him by the hair...

If the small-time trader Ilya Mironov had been alive now, Tikhon Ilyich would have fed the old man out of charity and wouldn't have known him, would scarcely have noticed him. After all, it had been like that with his mother; ask him now: do you remember your mother?

– and he'd reply: I remember some bent old woman… she dried dung, stoked the stove, drank in secret, grumbled… And nothing more. He had worked for Matorin for almost ten years, but those ten years had merged into a day or two as well: a light April rain is starting to fall and putting spots on the iron sheeting which they are flinging, with a crashing and a ringing, onto a cart beside the neighbouring store… a grey, frosty midday, pigeons are descending onto the snow in a noisy flock beside the store of the other neighbour, who trades in flour, groats and bran for livestock – they are flocking, cooing, with their wings a-tremble – while he and his brother are using an oxtail to whip a top, humming by the doorstep… Matorin was young then, strong, purple in the face, with a clean-shaven chin and ginger side whiskers, cut back halfway. Now he had grown poor, and with his old man's gait, in his sun-bleached *chuika* and deep cap, he rushed up and down from store to store, from acquaintance to acquaintance, played draughts, sat in Dayev's tavern having a drop to drink, getting tipsy and repeatedly saying:

"We're little people: we have a drink, a bite to eat, we settle up – and home!"

And on meeting Tikhon Ilyich, he does not recognize him and smiles pitifully:

"Can it be you, Tisha?"

And at their first meeting this autumn, Tikhon Ilyich had failed to recognize his own brother: "Is that really the Kuzma I roamed around with for so many years, over fields, through villages, down country roads?"

"You've aged, brother!"

"I have, a bit."

"And pretty early!"

"That's what being Russian means. It comes upon us quickly!"

Lighting a third cigarette, Tikhon Ilyich gazed doggedly and enquiringly out of the window.

"Is it the same in other countries too?"

No, it can't be. Some of his acquaintances had been abroad – the merchant Rukavishnikov, for example – and had talked about it… And you don't need Rukavishnikov to grasp it. Just take Russian Germans or Jews: they all conduct themselves in a businesslike, tidy way, they all know each other, they're all friends – and not only when they're getting drunk – they all help each other; if they move away from one another they correspond, they pass pictures of fathers, mothers, acquaintances from family to family; they teach their children, love them, go for walks with them, talk as if with equals – and so the child will have something to remember. Whereas with us Russians, everyone is everyone else's enemy, we're envious scandal-mongers, we visit each other once a year, we tear around like madmen when somebody drops in unexpectedly, we rush to tidy our rooms… And that's not all! We begrudge the guest a spoonful of jam! The guest won't have one extra glass without your begging him…

Someone's troika went past the window. Tikhon Ilyich examined it carefully. Lean horses, but evidently fast. The tarantass in good repair. Whose could it be? Nobody in the neighbourhood had such a troika. The neighbourhood gentry were such a poor lot, they went without bread for three days at a time, they'd sold the last rizas from their icons, they had no money to replace broken window panes or mend the roof; they stopped up the windows with pillows and put trays and buckets on the floor when it rained – it poured through the ceilings like through sieves… Then Deniska the cobbler walked by. Where was he going? And what with? Not with a suitcase? Oh what a fool, forgive me, Lord, my trespass!

Tikhon Ilyich shoved his feet mechanically into galoshes and went out onto the porch. Having gone out and taken a deep breath of the fresh air of the bluish, pre-winter dusk, he stopped again and sat down on the bench… Yes, now there was a family too – Grey and his son! Mentally, Tikhon Ilyich made the journey through the mud which Deniska had completed with a suitcase in his hand. He saw Durnovka, his estate, the gully, the huts, the dusk, his brother's light and lights in the homesteads… Kuzma was sitting and reading, no doubt. Bride was standing in the cold, dark hall, beside the barely warm stove, warming her hands and back, waiting for the word "dinner!" to be said and, pursing her aged, dried lips, thinking… Of what? Of Rodka? It was lies, all that about her having poisoned him, lies! But if she did poison him… Good Lord! If she did poison him – what must she feel? What a gravestone lying on her open soul!

Mentally, he glanced at Durnovka from the porch of his Durnovka home, at the black huts along the hillside beyond the gully, at the threshing barns and willows in the backyards… On the horizon beyond the fields to the left is the railway trackman's hut. A train passes by it in the dusk – a speeding row of fiery eyes. And then eyes light up in the huts. It grows darker, becomes cosier – and an unpleasant feeling stirs every time you glance at the huts of Bride and Grey, standing almost in the middle of Durnovka, three homesteads away from one another: there is no light in either the one or the other. Grey's little children are going blind, like moles, they go wild with joy and amazement when, on some happy evening, the hut can be lit up...

"No, it's a sin!" said Tikhon Ilyich firmly, and he rose from his seat. "No, it's unchristian! I must help, at least a little," he said, heading towards the station.

It was getting frosty, the smell of the samovar coming from the station was more fragrant. The lights there shone clearer, the bells on the troika jingled resonantly. A really nice little troika! Whereas it was a shame to look at the wretched horses of the peasant carriers, their tiny little carts on crooked wheels, falling to pieces and plastered with mud! The station door squealed and banged dully beyond the garden at the front. Skirting round it, Tikhon Ilyich climbed up onto the high stone porch, on which a two-bucket copper samovar was gurgling, its grille reddening like fiery teeth, and he bumped into just the person he wanted to – Deniska.

With his head lowered, deep in thought, Deniska was standing on the porch and holding in his right hand a cheap little grey suitcase, generously dotted with tin nail heads and tied up with a rope. Deniska was wearing a *poddyovka*, old and evidently very heavy, with drooping shoulders and a very low waist, a new cap and worn-out boots. He hadn't come out well height-wise, his legs were very short compared with his trunk. Now, with the low waist and worn-down boots, his legs seemed even shorter.

"Denis?" Tikhon Ilyich called. "What are you here for, you ruffian?"

Deniska, who was never surprised at anything, calmly raised his long-lashed eyes, dark and languid and sadly smiling, and pulled his cap off his hair. His hair was mousy-coloured and immoderately thick, his face sallow and as though oiled, but the eyes were beautiful.

"Hello, Tikhon Ilyich," he replied in a melodious little urban tenor, and, as always, as though shyly. "I'm going to... what's it... to Tula."

"And why's that, may I ask?"

"P'raps some job might come of it..."

49

Tikhon Ilyich examined him. In his hand there's the suitcase, poking out of a pocket of the *poddyovka* are some green and red booklets rolled into a tube. The *poddyovka*...

"You're no Tula dandy!"

Deniska examined himself as well.

"The *poddyovka*?" he asked modestly. "Well, I'll get some money in Tula and I'll buy myself a *venderka*. I seemed to do all right in the summer! Sold newspapers."

Tikhon Ilyich nodded at the suitcase:

"And what sort of a thing is that?

Deniska lowered his lashes:

"I bought myself a shootcase."

"Well you certainly can't go wearing a *vengerka** without a suitcase!" said Tikhon Ilyich mockingly. "And what's that in your pocket?"

"Just various rubbish..."

"Show me."

Deniska put the suitcase down on the porch and pulled the booklets out of his pocket. Tikhon Ilyich took them and looked through them carefully. A songbook, *Marusya*; *The Profligate Wife*; *An Innocent Girl in Chains of Violence*; *Congratulatory Verse for Parents, Educators and Benefactors*; *The Role*...

Here Tikhon Ilyich hesitated, but Deniska, who had been following him, was quick to prompt modestly:

"*The Role of the Protaleriat in Russia.*"

Tikhon Ilyich shook his head.

"That's something new! Nothing to eat, but you're buying suitcases and books. And what books! I suppose it's not for nothing they call you a trouble-maker. They say you're always slandering the Tsar? Watch out, brother!"

"I didn't go buying an estate, did I?" replied Deniska with a sad smile. "And I've never mentioned the Tsar. They lie about me as if I was dead. But I never even had it in my thoughts. Some sort of lunatic, am I?"

The pulley on the door began squealing, and the station watchman appeared – a grey-haired retired soldier, so short of breath he whistled and wheezed – and the buffet-keeper – fat, with bloated little eyes and greasy hair.

"Stand aside now, gentlemen merchants, allow us to take the samovar..."

Deniska stood aside and again took hold of the handle of the suitcase.

"I suppose you nicked it somewhere?" asked Tikhon Ilyich, nodding towards the suitcase and thinking of the business which had brought him to the station.

Deniska remained silent with his head bent.

"And it's empty, isn't it?"

Deniska burst out laughing:

"It is…"

"Have you been turned out of your job?"

"I left myself."

Tikhon Ilyich sighed.

"The living image of your father!" he said. "He was always like that as well: they'd give it him in the neck, and he'd say 'I left myself'."

"Strike me blind if I'm lying."

"Well, all right, all right… Have you been at home?"

"Two weeks."

"Is your father without work again?"

"He is without work noo."

"Noo!" Tikhon Ilyich mimicked him. "Country bumpkin! But a revolootionary too. Want to be a wolf, but with a dog's tail."

"And I reckon you're from that same stock," thought Deniska with a little grin, keeping his head down.

"And so Grey's just sitting there smoking?"

"He's a worthless fellow," said Deniska with conviction.

Tikhon Ilyich tapped him on the head with his knuckles.

"You might at least not display your foolishness! Who ever talks like that about his father?"

"The dog may be old, but I can't call him Dad," Deniska answered calmly. "If you're a father, provide food. And did he ever give me much to eat?"

But Tikhon Ilyich had stopped listening. He was choosing a convenient moment to begin talking business. And not listening, he interrupted:

"What a windbag you are… And have you got the money for the ticket to Tula?"

"What do I need that, a ticket, for?" replied Deniska. "When I get in the carriage, I'll be straight under a seat, God bless me. I've only got to get to Uzlovaya."

"And where are you going to read through your booklets? You won't get a lot read under a seat."

Deniska had a think.

"That's it!" he said. "Not under the seat all the time. I'll slip into the toilet, and you can read till daybreak if you want."

Tikhon Ilyich shifted his brows.

"Well, look here," he began. "Look here: it's time you changed the tune. You're not a kid, you idiot. Be off with you, back to Durnovka – it's time you got down to some work. Because it makes me sick, you know, looking at you lot. At my place... the courtyard counsellors live better. So be it, then, I'll help... to begin with. Well, to buy bits of goods, or tools... And at least you'll be feeding yourself and giving your father a little..."

"What is it he's leading up to?" thought Deniska.

And Tikhon Ilyich made up his mind and concluded:

"And it's time you got married too."

"So-o!" thought Deniska, and unhurriedly began rolling a cigarette.

"Well," he responded, calmly and a little sadly, without raising his lashes. "I wouldn't think of being stubborn. Marriage is a possibility. It's worse going to prestitutes."

"Well, that's just it," Tikhon Ilyich chimed in. "Only bear it in mind, brother – you have to get married sensibly. It's a good thing to breed them, children, that is, with some capital."

Deniska burst into loud laughter.

"What are you cackling about?"

"What do you think? Breed them! Like chickens or pigs?"

"They want food no less than chickens and pigs."

"And married to who?" Deniska asked with a sad grin.

"Who to? To... whoever you like."

"It's to that Bride, is it?"

Tikhon Ilyich blushed deeply.

"Idiot! And what's wrong with Bride? She's a meek woman, hard-working..."

Deniska was silent for a while, picking at a tin nail head on the suitcase with his fingernail. Then he pretended to be stupid.

"There's lots of them brides," he drawled. "I don't know which one you're nattering about... Is it the one you used to live with?"

But Tikhon Ilyich had already recovered himself.

"Whether I did or not is nothing to do with you, you swine," he replied, and so quickly and convincingly that Deniska mumbled submissively:

"No, it'd only be an honour for me... I was just saying... by the way..."

"Well then, don't talk rubbish to no end. I'll give you a start in life. Got it? I'll provide a dowry... Got it?"

Deniska fell deep into thought.

"When I get back from Tula..." he began.

"The cockerel's found a pearl! What the devil do you need Tula for?"

"I've got so hungry at home..."

Tikhon Ilyich threw open his *chuika*, thrust his hand into a pocket of his *poddyovka*, and all but resolved upon giving Deniska a twenty-kopek piece. But he had a sudden thought – it's stupid chucking money about, and this pushy kid'll be giving himself airs, thinking, like, I'm being bribed – and he pretended he was searching for something.

"Oh dear, forgotten my cigarettes! Let me roll one."

Deniska handed him his tobacco pouch. The lantern over the porch had already been lit, and by its dim light Tikhon Ilyich read out loud what was boldly embroidered in white thread on the pouch:

"A prezent for him I ador to show I do ador this pouch a gift for ever more."

"Neat!" he said, after reading it.

Deniska cast his eyes down shyly.

"So you already have a sweetheart, then?"

"There's no shortage of bitches knocking about!" Deniska replied carelessly. "But I'm not refusing to get married. I'll be back after Christmas-tide, and Lord bless me..."

A cart began rumbling from beyond the garden, and it drove up to the porch with a clatter; it was all bespattered with mud, with a little peasant perched on its edge and the Ulyanovka deacon, Govorov, in the straw in the middle.

"Has it gone?" the deacon cried in alarm, throwing a foot in a new galosh out of the straw.

Every hair of his gingery-red, shaggy head curled ungovernably, his hat had slipped to the back of his head, and his face was all aglow from the wind and agitation.

"The train?" asked Tikhon Ilyich. "No, sir, it's not pulled out yet, sir."

"Aha! Well, thank God!" the deacon exclaimed joyfully, and all the same, leaping out of the cart, he hurled himself headlong towards the doors.

"Well, so be it then," said Tikhon Ilyich. "Till after Christmas, then."

Inside the station it smelt of wet sheepskin jackets, the samovar, cheap tobacco and paraffin. The air was so smoky that it grated on the throat and the lamps barely gave any light in the smoke, the semi-darkness, the damp and the cold. Doors squealed and slammed, and peasants with knouts in their hands jostled and made a racket – these were cab-drivers from Ulyanovka who sometimes waited a week at a time for a fare. Walking among them with his eyebrows raised was a Jewish corn merchant in a bowler hat and hooded overcoat and with an umbrella on his shoulder. Beside the ticket office some peasants were dragging their master's suitcases and baskets with oilcloth sewn round them onto the scales, and shouting at them was the telegraphist and acting assistant station manager – a short-legged young fellow with a large head and a curly yellow quiff, fluffed up from under his cap on the left temple in Cossack style – and sitting shivering violently on the dirty floor was a pointer, spotted like a frog and with mournful eyes.

Pushing his way through the peasants, Tikhon Ilyich went up to the buffet counter and had a chat with the tender. Then he set off to go back home. Deniska was still standing on the porch.

"What I wanted to ask you, Tikhon Ilyich," he said, even more shyly than ever.

"What is it now?" Tikhon Ilyich asked angrily. "Money? I shan't give you any."

"No, what money! To read my letter."

"Letter? Who to?"

"To you. I wanted to give it you before, but couldn't pluck up the courage."

"And what about?"

"Well… I've described how I've been living…"

Tikhon Ilyich took the scrap of paper from Deniska's hands, shoved it into his pocket and strode off home across the springy, hardened mud.

Now he was in a manly mood. He wanted some work to do, and he thought with pleasure that the livestock would need feeding again. It was a pity – he'd got heated, thrown Seedcake out, and now he'd have to go without a night's sleep himself. There was no relying on Oska. He was probably already asleep. Or else he was sitting with the cook and bad-mouthing the master... And after passing by the lighted windows of the hut, Tikhon Ilyich stole into the lobby and pressed his ear up against the door. Laughter came from the other side of the door, then Oska's voice:

"Or else here's another thing that happened. There was a peasant living in the village – ever so, ever so poor, there was none poorer in all the world. And this peasant rode out once, my brothers, ploughing. And a spotted dog trailed after him. The peasant's ploughing, and the dog's belting around the field and keeps on trying to dig something up. It dug and dug, and then simply how-owled! What's going on, then? The peasant rushes over to it, looks into the pit, and there it is – an iron pot..."

"An iron po-ot?" asked the cook.

"Just you listen. An iron pot it may have been, but in that pot there was gold! Huge amounts... Well, and the peasant got rich..."

"Oh, the gasbags!" thought Tikhon Ilyich, but he began listening avidly to what would happen to the peasant next.

"The peasant got rich, built himself a house, like some merchant..."

"No worse than our Tightlegs," interjected the cook.

Tikhon Ilyich grinned: he knew they'd been calling him Tightlegs for a long time now... There's none without a nickname!

But Oska continued:

"A bit richer even... Yes... But the dog's gone and died. What should he do? He's really sorry about the dog, it's got to be properly buried..."

An explosion of chuckling rang out. The narrator himself started to chuckle, and so did someone else too – with an old man's cough.

"Can that be Seedcake?" Tikhon Ilyich jerked up. "Well, thank God. I told the idiot, didn't I: you-ou'll be back!"

"The peasant went to the priest," Oska continued, "went to the priest, and he goes: 'Father, the dog's died – it's got to be buried—'"

Again the cook could not contain herself and cried joyfully:

"Oh, you'll be the death of me!"

"Let me finish, now!" Oska cried too, and again went back to his narrative tone, imitating now the priest, now the peasant:

"So he goes: 'Father, the dog's got to be buried.' And the priest just starts stamping his feet: 'What do you mean, buried? Bury the dog in the graveyard? I'll leave you to rot in jail, I'll have you put in irons!' – 'But Father, that isn't just an ordinary dog, you know: as it was dying, it left you five hundred roubles!' The priest just leaps up from his seat: 'Idiot! Do you think I'm scolding you about it getting buried? I'm scolding you about *where* it gets buried! It's got to be buried inside the church fence!'"

Tikhon Ilyich coughed loudly and opened the door. At the table, beside a smoking lamp, the broken glass of which was stuck together on one side with a blackened bit of paper, there sat the cook with her head bent down and her whole face curtained with wet hair. She was combing her hair with a wooden comb and examining the comb against the light through her hair. Oska, with a cigarette in his teeth, was leaning back chuckling with his bast shoes dangling. Beside the stove, in semi-darkness, was a little red light – a pipe. When Tikhon Ilyich jerked the door and appeared on the threshold, the chuckling was immediately broken off, and the man smoking the pipe meekly rose from his seat, took the pipe out of his mouth and shoved it into his pocket... Yes, it was Seedcake! But as if nothing at all had happened in the morning, Tikhon Ilyich cried cheerfully and amicably:

"Lads! Time to feed the animals..."

They wandered around the farmyard with a lantern, lighting up the hardened dung, the scattered straw, the mangers and the posts, throwing huge shadows and waking the chickens on their perches beneath the awnings. The chickens flew off, dropped down, and, leaning forward, ran in any direction, falling asleep as they ran. The large, purple eyes of the horses, which turned their heads to the light, gleamed and looked strange and magnificent. Steam came from their breathing – as though they were all smoking. And whenever Tikhon Ilyich lowered the lantern and glanced upwards, with joy he would see, in the deep, clear sky above the square of the yard, the bright, multicoloured stars. The north wind could be heard rustling drily over the roofs and blowing frosty freshness into the cracks... Thank the Lord, it's winter!

Finishing his chores and ordering the samovar, Tikhon Ilyich went with the lantern into the cold, fragrant store and chose one of the better pickled herrings: "It's no bad thing to have something a bit salty before tea!" – and he ate it with his tea, drank several glasses of bitter-sweet, yellow-red rowan-berry vodka, poured a cup of tea, found Deniska's letter in his pocket and started deciphering the scribbles.

"Denya got forty roobles of munny then gathered his things…"

"Forty!" thought Tikhon Ilyich. "Oh, the ragamuffin!"

"Denya went to Tula stashun and rite there he was robbed they took it all to the last kopek there was noware to go and Angwish took him…"

It was difficult and dull deciphering this rubbish, but the evening was long, and he had nothing to do… The samovar was seething restlessly, the lamp shone with a calm light – and in the peace and quiet of the evening there was sadness. The rattle was going rhythmically outside the windows, putting out a ringing dance tune in the frosty air…

"Then I got mizrable how am I to go home my father's really scary…"

"What an idiot, forgive me, Lord!" thought Tikhon Ilyich. "Grey – scary?"

"I'll go into the thick forest and pick a big fir and take a rope from the shoogar loaf to assine myself to the life itternal in new trowsers but with noshoos…"

"With no shoes, is that?" said Tikhon Ilyich, moving the paper away from his tired eyes. "Now that's true all right…"

Tossing the letter into the slop bucket, he put his elbows onto the table and gazed at the lamp… We're a strange people! What a motley soul! One moment a man's an absolute dog, the next he's mournful, grieving, self-indulgent, crying over himself… there you have the likes of Deniska or him himself, Tikhon Ilyich… The window panes were misted over, the rattle was uttering something nice in a distinct and lively, wintry way… Oh dear, if only he had children! If only he had – well, a mistress, perhaps, instead of that dumpy old woman who got on your nerves just with her stories about the Princess and some devout nun Polikarpia, who's called Polly-Copier in town! But it was too late, too late.

Undoing the embroidered collar of his shirt, with a bitter smile Tikhon Ilyich fingered his neck, the hollows down the neck behind the ears... Those hollows were the first sign of old age – the head getting horselike! And the rest wasn't bad either. He bent his head and thrust his fingers into his beard... And his beard was grey, dry and tangled. No, that's enough, that's enough, Tikhon Ilyich!

He drank, got tipsy, and squeezed his jaws ever tighter as he stared ever harder, screwing up his eyes, at the wick of the lamp, burning with an even flame... Just think: he can't go and visit his own brother – the boars won't let him, the swine! And even if they did let him, there'd be no great joy either. Kuzma would lecture him, Bride would stand with her lips pursed and her lashes lowered... Those lowered eyes alone were enough to make you run away!

His heart ached, there was a fog in his head... Where was it he'd heard that song?

> On came my boring evening,
> And started to depress me,
> In came my darling lover,
> And started to caress me...

Ah yes, it was in Lebedyan, at the inn. The lace-makers sit singing on a winter's evening... They sit there plaiting and, without raising their lashes, they give out in ringing, chesty voices:

> With kisses and embraces,
> He bids a fond farewell...

There was a fog in his head – one moment everything would seem to be ahead of him still – joy, and freedom, and light-heartedness – and then his heart would again begin aching hopelessly. One moment he would say:

"While there's money in your pocket, there's a woman who'll do business!"

Then he would gaze bad-temperedly at the lamp and, having his brother in mind, mutter:

"A teacher! A preacher! Philaret the Murkyful!* The bloody ragamuffin!"

He finished off the rowan-berry vodka, smoked so much it grew dark... Stepping unsteadily over the uneven floor, he went out into the dark lobby in just his jacket, sensed the powerful freshness of the air, the smell of the straw, the smell of the dogs, and he saw two greenish lights flashing on the doorstep...

"Buyan!" he called.

And with all his might he struck Buyan on the head with his boot.

A deathly quiet reigned over the earth, which was softly black in the starry light. Multicoloured patterns of stars were gleaming. The highway was faintly white, vanishing in the twilight. In the distance, a growing rumbling could be heard, muffled, as if from beneath the earth. And suddenly it burst out onto the surface and started droning all around: with its gleaming white chain of windows lit up by electricity, like a flying witch, scattering braids of smoke, illumined with scarlet light from below, an express was rushing along in the distance, cutting across the highway...

"It's going past Durnovka!" said Tikhon Ilyich, hiccupping. "Past Grey! Ah, the thieves, the devils..."

The sleepy cook came into his room, dimly lit by the dying lamp and stinking of tobacco, and brought in a greasy little cast-iron pot of cabbage soup she had picked up with old cloths, black with grease and soot. Tikhon Ilyich looked at her askance and said:

"Get out of here this minute."

The cook turned, kicked the door open and disappeared.

Then he picked up Gattsuk's calendar,* dipped a rusty pen into the rusty ink and, clenching his teeth and gazing sleepily with leaden eyes, began writing endlessly in all directions across the calendar:

"Gattsuk Gattsuk Gattsuk Gattsuk..."

2

K UZMA HAD DREAMT ALL HIS LIFE of studying and writing. Poetry was nothing! He was only "fooling around" with poetry. He wanted to recount the way he was perishing, to depict with unprecedented mercilessness his poverty and the way of life, terrible in its ordinariness, that was crippling him, making him a fruitless fig tree.

Pondering on his life, he both chastised and vindicated himself.

Why, his story is the story of all self-taught Russians. He was born in a country that has more than a hundred million illiterates. He grew up in the Chornaya Sloboda, where even now men are beaten to death in fist fights, amid great savagery and the most profound ignorance. He and Tikhon were taught their letters and numbers by a neighbour, Belkin the galosh-mender; and even that was only because he never had any work – who ever heard of galoshes in the Sloboda! – because it was always nice to give someone's "locks" a tug, and because you couldn't spend all the time sitting beltless on the *zavalinka*, bending over with your shaggy head laid bare to the sun and spitting every now and then onto the dust between your bare feet. In Matorin's market store the brothers got the hang of reading and writing, and Kuzma began to be keen on books too, which he was given by the market's freethinker and eccentric, the old accordion-player Balashkin. But there was no time for reading in the store! Matorin very often shouted: "I'll give yer ears a good boxing fer yer Psacs,* you little devil you!"

Kuzma started writing there too – he began with a story about how a merchant was travelling through the Murom forests in a dreadful storm in the night, found himself a place to sleep with some robbers and had his throat cut. Kuzma fervently set forth his dying prayers, his thoughts, his grief over his iniquitous life, "so soon cut short..." But the market doused him in cold water without mercy:

"What an idiot you are, forgive me Lord! 'So soon'! It was high time for the pot-bellied devil! And how was it you found out what he was thinking, then? They cut his throat, didn't they?"

Then Kuzma wrote a song in the style of Koltsov of an aged knight, bequeathing his faithful steed to his son. "He bore me in my youthful days!" the knight exclaimed in the song.

"So!" they said to him. "How old was that there steed then? Ah, Kuzma, Kuzma! You'd do better writing something serious – well, maybe about the war, for instance..."

And Kuzma, adapting himself to the market's taste, started writing about what the market was then talking about – the Russo-Turkish War: how

> Eighteen sev'nty-seven came,
> Now the Turk looked for a fight,
> He sent his horde advancing,
> Tried to conquer Russia's might,

and how that horde

> Wearing ugly little caps,
> Sneaked up on the Tsar of Cannons...

He realized with great pain later on what obtuseness and ignorance there was in such doggerel and the worth of that loutish language, that Russian contempt for foreign caps!

Leaving the store and selling what remained after the death of their mother, they set up as small-time traders. They often happened to be in their native town, and Kuzma was friendly with Balashkin as before, and avidly read the books which Balashkin gave him or suggested. However, at the same time as he was talking with Balashkin about Schiller, he was dreaming passionately of persuading him to lend him a "squeeze box". While rhapsodizing about *Smoke*,* he said repeatedly, however, that "he who is clever, but not learned, without learning has much light". After visiting Koltsov's grave, in rapture he made a note of the illiterate inscription on its stone: "*Beneath this monument is buried the body of the Voronezh townsman and poet alesei vasilyevich Kaltsov endowed by the grace of the monarch with the nature of a man enlightened without lessens...*"

Old, huge, thin, never removing winter or summer the *chuika* that had turned green or his warm cap, large-faced, clean-shaven and crooked-mouthed, Balashkin could be almost frightening with his angry speeches, with his deep, old man's bass, with the prickly, silvery stubble on his grey cheeks, and his green left eye bulging, flashing and squinting to the side to which his mouth was asquint as well. And how he bellowed one day, after listening to a speech from Kuzma about "enlightenment without lessons", how he flashed that eye, tossing away the cigarette which he had been filling with cheap tobacco over an empty box of sprats!

"Donkey jaw! What's this rot you're talking? Have you considered what this 'enlightenment without lessons' of ours means?"

And he seized the cigarette again and began a muffled roaring:

"Mercibul God! They killed Pushkin, they killed Lermontov; they drowned Pisarev, they hanged Ryleyev… They dragged Dostoevsky off to be shot, they drove Gogol out of his mind… And Shevchenko? And Polezhayev?* You reckon the government's to blame? But you can tell the master by his man, people get what they deserve. Oh, and in all the world is there another country such as this, a race such as this, may it be thrice accursed?"

Pulling uneasily at the buttons of his long-skirted frock coat, first doing himself up, then undoing himself, the embarrassed Kuzma, frowning and smirking, said in reply:

"A race such as this! A very great race, and not one 'such as this', permit me to point out to you."

"Don't you dare to hand out prizes!" cried Balashkin again.

"No, sir, I shall dare! After all, those writers are the children of that same race. Platon Karatayev* – there's the acknowledged typical man of that race!"

"And why not Yeroshka, why not Lukashka? If I want to give literature a shake, brother, I'll find boots to fit all the gods! Why Karatayev, but not Razuvayev and Kolupayev, not the bloodsucking spider, not the extortionist priest, not the corrupt clerk, not some Saltychikha or other, not Karamazov or Oblomov, not Khlestakov or Nozdryov,* or, so as not to go too far afield, not your good-for-nothing brother?"

"Platon Karatayev…"

"To hell with your lousy Karatayev! I don't see any ideal there!"

"And the Russian martyrs, zealots, saints and holy fools living on alms, the schismatics?"

"Wha-at? And the Coliseums, the Crusades, the lerigious wars, the countless sects? And Luther, what's more, you know? No, don't try it on with me! You won't get the better of me so easily!"

Yes, one thing was required – to study. But when, where?

Five whole years of trading – and at the very best time of life! Even a trip to town seemed great good fortune. A rest, acquaintances, the smell of bakeries and iron roofs, the cobblestones on Torgovaya Street, tea, white bread and the Persian march in the Kars tavern... The earthen floors in the stores, sprinkled with water from kettles, the warbling of the famous quail at Rudakov's doors, the smell of the fish stalls, dill, Romanov's cheap tobacco... Balashkin's kind, ugly smile at the sight of the approaching Kuzma... Then – thundering and cursing at the Slavophiles, Belinsky* and foul-mouthed abuse, the disjointed, passionate throwing of names and quotations at one another... And the most hopeless conclusions – in the end. "And it really is over and done with now – we're hurtling flat out back to Asia!" the old man would drone, and suddenly, lowering his voice, he would look around: "Have you heard? They say Saltykov's dying.* The last one! They've poisoned him, they say..." And in the morning – again the cart, the steppe, baking heat or mud, intensely agonizing reading to the bumps of the turning wheels... Long contemplation of the far-reaching steppe, the sweetly mournful melody of poetry in the soul, interrupted by thoughts of earnings or by a slanging match with Tikhon... The exciting smell of the road – of dust and tar... The smell of mint spice cakes and the suffocating stench of cats' pelts from the trunk on the cart... Those years had truly worn him out – the shirts not taken off for two weeks at a time, the cold, dry food, the limping because of lopsided boots, and the heels battered till they bled, the nights spent in strangers' huts and lobbies!

Kuzma crossed himself with a flourish when he finally slipped out of that bondage. But again he had to earn a crust of bread somehow. After working for next to no time for a cattle-dealer near Yelets, he made for Voronezh. He had long ago begun a love affair in Voronezh, a liaison with another man's wife – and it was to there he was drawn. And for almost ten years he hung around in Voronezh – around the grain-collecting station, brokering and writing occasional little articles in the newspapers about the grain business, gratifying, or rather, tormenting his soul with Tolstoy's articles, Schedrin's satires. And was constantly wracked by the persistent thought that his life was being, had already been wasted.

At the beginning of the '90s Balashkin died of a hernia, and Kuzma saw him for the last time not long before. And what a meeting it was!

"I have to write," complained one, sullen and bad-tempered. "Or else you wither like burdock in a field…"

"Yes, yes," droned the other, already squinting his benumbed eye sleepily, moving his jaw with difficulty and unable to get the tobacco into his cigarette. "It's said: learn ev'ry hour, think ev'ry hour… just look around – at all our woes and wretchedness…"

Then he gave a bashful grin, put the cigarette aside and put his hand into the table drawer.

"Here," he muttered, rummaging in a bundle of well-rubbed papers of some sort and cuttings from newspapers. "Here's a lot of good stuff, my friend… I've been continually reading, and cutting out and making notes… When I die, it'll be of use to you – devilish material about Russian life. But hang on now, there's one little story I'll find for you in a moment…"

But he rummaged and rummaged and failed to find it, he started searching for his glasses, started fumbling uneasily in his pockets – and gave it up as a bad job. And on doing so, knitted his brows and began shaking his head:

"No, no – don't even dare touch that for the time being. You're still a feeble-minded ignoramus. Don't bite off more than you can chew. On that topic, what I gave you about Sukhonosov, have you written it? Not yet? Well and what a donkey jaw! What a topic!"

"About the village, it should be, about the people," said Kuzma. "I mean, you say it yourself: Russia, Russia…"

"And isn't Drynose the people, Russia? *The whole of it's a village, get that into your head once and for all!* Look around you: is this a town, in your opinion? There's a herd barging through the streets ev'ry evening – you can't see your neighbour for the dust… And you call it 'a town'."

Sukhonosov, Drynose… For many a year that vile old man from the Chornaya Sloboda, whose entire property consisted of a straw mattress soiled by bedbugs and a moth-eaten coat inherited from his wife, never left Kuzma's head. He lived by begging, he was hungry and ill, for fifty kopeks a month he rented a bed from a woman from the food stalls in the market and, in her view, could have made an excellent improvement to his circumstances by selling his inheritance. But he valued it as the apple of his eye – and, of course, not at all on the strength of any tender feelings for the deceased: it made him conscious that he did have, unlike others, property. He thought that it was devilishly expensive: "They just don't make coats like that nowadays." He was not averse, not at all averse to selling it. But he demanded such ridiculous prices that the buyers were left open-mouthed... And Kuzma understood this Sloboda tragedy very well. But, on beginning to consider how to put it all down, he began going over the whole, complex life of the Sloboda, memories of his childhood, his youth – and he got entangled, he drowned Sukhonosov in the wealth of pictures besieging his imagination, and he lost heart, overwhelmed by the need to express his own soul, to reveal everything that was crippling his own life. And the most terrible thing of all in that life was that it was simple, humdrum, and was being squandered on trifles with incomprehensible speed...

Not a few more fruitless years had passed since that time. He was a broker in Voronezh, then, when the woman he lived with died in a puerperal fever, he was a broker in Yelets, he worked in a candle store in Lipetsk, he was a clerk on Kasatkin's estate. He became for a time a passionate adherent of Tolstoy: for about a year he did not smoke, did not touch vodka, did not eat meat, never parted with *Confession* or the *Gospels*,* and he wanted to resettle in the Caucasus with the Dukhobors...* But then he was ordered to Kiev for a while on business. It was a clear end to September, everything was cheerful, splendid: the clean air, the heatless sunshine, the speed of the train, the open windows and the colourful woods flashing past them... During the stop at Nezhin, Kuzma suddenly saw a large crowd by the doors of the station. The crowd had surrounded somebody and was shouting, getting agitated, arguing. Kuzma's heart began pounding and he ran over to the crowd. He pushed his way through quickly – and saw the red cap of the stationmaster and the grey greatcoat of a strapping gendarme, who was berating three Ukrainian peasants; they stood submissively, but stubbornly before him, wearing short, thick coats, indestructible boots and brown sheepskin hats. Those hats barely sat on some terrible things – round heads bound with gauze, roughened by dried blood, above bulbous eyes and swollen, glassy faces covered in greenish-yellow bruises and dried-up, blackened wounds: the

Ukrainians had been bitten by a rabid wolf and sent to a clinic in Kiev, and they were sitting for days at almost every big station without bread and without so much as a kopek. And learning they were not being allowed to leave now, solely because this train was called a fast one, Kuzma flew into a sudden rage and, to the approving cries of the Jews in the crowd, he started yelling and stamping his feet at the gendarme. He was detained, a report was drawn up, and, while waiting for the next train, he drank himself into oblivion.

The Ukrainians were from Chernigov Province. He had always pictured it as a godforsaken land, with a dull, overcast blue above the woods. These people, who had come through mortal combat with a rabid beast, reminded him of the times of Prince Vladimir,* of a bygone life that was lived in the forests, the ancient life of the peasant. And as he got drunk, pouring out a glass with hands that were shaking after the rowdy scene, Kuzma was in raptures: "Ah, and what a time it was!" He choked with anger at both the gendarme and the submissive cattle in their thick coats. Obtuse and savage, curse them... But it's Rus, ancient Rus! And Kuzma's eyes were dimmed by tears of drunken joy and strength which distorted any picture to unnatural dimensions. "And non-resistance?" he remembered at times, and shook his head, smirking. With his back towards him at the common table, a nice, clean young officer was having dinner, and Kuzma looked with gentle insolence at his white tunic, so short and with such a high waist that he wanted to go over and pull it down. "And I shall!" thought Kuzma. "And if he leaps up and shouts – one in the mug! And there's non-resistance for you..." Later he went on to Kiev and, without bothering about his business, he spent three days, tipsy and joyously excited, walking around the town and along the steep heights above the Dnieper. And at mass in St Sophia's Cathedral many people stared in astonishment at the thin Russian standing before Prince Yaroslav's sarcophagus.* His appearance was strange: mass was finishing, the people were leaving, the sextons were extinguishing the candles, but he, with gritted teeth, with his sparse, greying beard lowered onto his chest, and his deep-sunken eyes closed in suffering and happiness, was listening to the bells pealing tunefully and indistinctly above the cathedral... And in the evening he was seen at the monastery. He sat next to a little crippled boy, who gazed with a sad and lacklustre smile at its white walls and the gold of its small cupolas in the autumnal sky. The little boy was hatless, with a canvas bag over his shoulder, wore dirty rags on his skinny body, held a little wooden cup with a kopek in the bottom in one hand, while with the other he kept changing the position, as if it were someone else's, as if it were a thing, of his misshapen right leg, bared to the knee, withered, unnaturally slender, tanned to black and overgrown with a golden coat. There was nobody around, but sleepily and painfully throwing back his cropped head, rough from the sun and dust, showing his slender, child's collarbones and paying no attention to the flies that preyed on his dripping nose, the little boy drawled incessantly:

Look, mothers,
how unfortunate we are, how we suffer!
Ah, the Lord forbid, mothers,
anyone should suffer so!

And Kuzma voiced his agreement: "Yes, yes! That's right!"

In Kiev he came to understand clearly that he would not last long with Kasatkin now, and that ahead there was poverty and the loss of his humanity. And so it was. He lasted for a little while longer, but in a very shameful and difficult position: eternally half-drunk, untidy, hoarse, impregnated through and through with cheap tobacco, hardly able to conceal his unfitness for work... Later on he fell even lower: he returned to his native town and ran through his last coppers; he slept the whole winter in the dormitory at Khodov's hostel, and killed the days in Avdeyich's tavern at the Babyi market. A lot of those coppers went on a silly venture – the publication of a book of poems – and afterwards he was obliged to roam among Avdeyich's customers and foist the book upon them at half-price... But as if that were not enough, he became a buffoon! Once he was standing beside the flour stalls at the market and watching a tramp contorting himself in front of the merchant Moszhukhin, who had come out onto his doorstep. The sleepily mocking Moszhukhin, with a face like a reflection in a samovar, was more interested in the cat which was licking his polished boot. But the tramp did not stop. He struck himself on the chest with his fist and, raising his shoulders and wheezing, began to declaim:

> He drinks when he's hung-over,
> For that's the wise man's sign...

And Kuzma, with his bulbous eyes gleaming, chimed in:

> So pass the bottle over,
> And long live beer and wine!

But an old townswoman who was passing, who had a face like an old lioness, she stopped, looked at him from under her brows and, raising her crutch, said distinctly, spitefully:

"I don't suppose you've learnt any prayers that well!"

He could sink no lower. But it was this that saved him. He suffered several terrible heart attacks – and immediately stopped the drinking, firmly resolving to begin the simplest life of labour, to rent orchards or allotments, for example...

This idea gladdened him. "Yes, yes," he thought, "it's high time!" And it was true, he needed a rest, a poor, but clean life. He had already started to age. His beard had turned completely grey, his hair, combed with a straight parting and curling at the ends, had thinned and acquired the colour of iron, his broad-cheekboned face had darkened and become even thinner...

In the spring, a few months before making peace with Tikhon, Kuzma heard that an orchard was to let in his native district, in the village of Kazakovo, and he hurried off to it.

It was the beginning of May; after some hot weather, cold and rain had set in; gloomy, autumnal storm clouds were passing over the town. Wearing an old *chuika* and an old cap, Kuzma was striding in worn-down boots to the station beyond Pushkarnaya Sloboda, and, with his arms folded behind him underneath his *chuika*, he was shaking his head and pulling a face because of the cigarette in his teeth, and smiling ironically: a barefooted little boy had just come running towards him with a pile of newspapers, and as he ran had called out cheerily the usual phrase:

"Gen'ral strike!"

"You're a bit late, young fellow," said Kuzma. "Is there nothing newer?"

The little boy paused with his eyes shining:

"The policeman took the new ones away at the station," he replied.

"What a constitution!" Kuzma said caustically and moved on, jumping over the mud beneath rotting fences, dark from the rain, beneath the boughs of the wet gardens and the windows of the crooked shacks stretching down the hill to the end of the town street. "Truly amazing!" he thought as he jumped. Formerly in such weather people had been yawning in stores and inns, hardly tossing one another a word. Now all over the town there was talk of the Duma, of revolts and fires, of how "Muromtsev had given the Prime Minister a ticking-off..."* Well, but a frog doesn't have a tail for long! In the town gardens a police band was playing... A whole regiment of Cossacks had been sent in... And three days before on Torgovaya Street, one of them had gone up drunk to the open window of the public library and, unbuttoning his trousers, had suggested the young lady librarian buy his "one plus two". An old cabman standing nearby had begun putting him to shame, and the Cossack had drawn his sabre, cut his shoulder open and rushed down the street with foul-mouthed abuse after the passers-by, who, mad with terror, had gone flying off helter-skelter...

"Cat-catcher, cat-catcher, too drunk to look at yer!" the shrill voices of some little girls howled after Kuzma as they jumped from stone to stone in the shallow Sloboda stream. "They're killing cats over there, you can go and get your share!"

"Ooh, you little wretches," they were scolded by the conductor walking ahead of Kuzma in a greatcoat that was terribly heavy even to look at. "Found someone of your own age, haven't you!"

But it was clear from his voice that he was containing his laughter. The conductor's old, deep galoshes were covered in dried mud, the half-belt of the greatcoat hung on a single button. The little log bridge he was crossing lay crooked. Further on, beside ditches rinsed out by the spring floods, grew some stunted willows. And Kuzma glanced cheerlessly both at them and at the straw roofs down the Sloboda hill, at the smoke-coloured and bluish clouds above them, and at a reddish dog gnawing a bone in a ditch...

"No, no," he thought, going up the hill. "A frog doesn't have a tail for long!" Reaching the top and catching sight of the red station buildings amidst empty green fields, he smirked again. A parliament, deputies! The day before he had returned from the gardens where, to mark a holiday, there had been illuminations, rockets had been going up, and the police band had played 'Toreador' and 'Beside the River, Beside the Bridge', 'Maxixe' and 'The Troika', crying out in the midst of the gallop: "Hey, my dear-ies!"; he had gone back and begun ringing at the gates of his hostel. He had tugged and tugged on the rattling wire – not a soul. Not a soul around either; the quiet, the twilight, the cold, greenish sky in the sunset behind the square at the end of the street, above his head – storm clouds... Finally someone comes trudging along inside the gates, groaning. Jangles the keys and mumbles:

"Gone completely lame..."

"Why's that?" asked Kuzma.

"Hit by a horse," answered the man as he opened up, and, throwing the side gate open, he added: "Well, two more left to come now."

"They're from the court, are they?"

"Yes."

"And do you know why the court's here?"

"To try a deputy... They say he wanted to poison the river."

"A deputy? You idiot, as if deputies do that sort of thing."

"Goodness knows..."

On the outskirts of the Sloboda beside the threshold of a clay hut stood a tall old man in down-at-heel shoes. In the old man's hand was a long hazel staff, and, seeing a passer-by, he made haste to pretend he was much older than he was – he grasped the staff with both hands, lifted his shoulders, pulled a tired, sad face. The damp, cold wind blowing from the fields ruffled the locks of his grey hair. And Kuzma remembered his father, childhood... "Rus, Rus! Where are you rushing to?" Gogol's exclamation* came into his head. "Rus, Rus!... Ah, you gasbags, you'll be the death of me! That would be more like it – 'a deputy wanted to poison the river'... Yes, but who are you going to call to account? The wretched people, first and foremost – the wretched people!..." And tears welled up in Kuzma's small green eyes – all of a sudden, as had begun to happen often of late. Not long ago he had wandered into Avdeyich's inn at the Babyi market. Had gone into the yard, drowning in ankle-deep mud, and had climbed from the yard to the first floor up such a stinking wooden staircase, rotten through and through, that even he, a man who had seen a few things in his time, had started feeling sick; with difficulty he had opened a heavy, greasy door, covered in shreds of felt, ripped rags instead of upholstery, and with a pulley made of a rope and a brick – and had been blinded

71

by tobacco smoke, and deafened by the clattering of crockery on the counter, the stamping of waiters running in all directions and the nasal clamour of the gramophone. Then he had gone through into the back room where there were fewer people, sat down at a table and asked for a bottle of mead... Beneath his feet on the trampled and spit-covered floor had been pieces of sucked lemon, eggshells, cigarette butts... And by the wall opposite had sat a lanky peasant in bast shoes, smiling blissfully, shaking his shaggy head, listening intently to the clamouring gramophone. On the table had been a hundred-gram carafe of vodka, a glass, some pretzels. But the peasant had not been drinking, only nodding his head, looking at his bast shoes, and suddenly, feeling Kuzma's gaze upon him, he had opened his joyful eyes, raised his wonderful, kind face with its ginger, curly beard. "I'm in seventh heaven!" he had exclaimed, joyfully and in amazement. And had hurried to add – in justification: "My brother works here, mister... My own brother..." And blinking away the tears, Kuzma had gritted his teeth. Ooh, the bastards, how they'd trampled the people down, cowed them! "Seventh heaven!" And that was about Avdeyich's! And as if that were not enough, when Kuzma had got up and said: "Well, so long!" the peasant had hurriedly got up too, and out of the fullness of his happy heart, with deep gratitude both for the luxury of the surroundings and for the fact that he had been spoken to in a decent manner, he had hurriedly replied: "Don't take umbrage..."

Previously people in train carriages had talked only about rains and droughts, about the fact that "grain prices are the work of God". Now newspaper pages rustled in the hands of many, and talk was again of the Duma, of liberties, the alienation of land; nobody even noticed the torrential rain rattling on the roofs, although the travellers were greedy for the spring rains – grain-merchants, peasants, townsmen from farmsteads. A young soldier with an amputated leg went by – suffering from jaundice, with black, sad eyes, he was hobbling, tapping with his wooden leg, doffing his Manchurian fur hat and, like a beggar, crossing himself at every offering of alms. And noisy, indignant talk arose about the government, about the minister Durnovo* and some state-owned oats... They recalled in mockery what they had previously delighted in: how, to frighten the Japanese at Portsmouth, "Vitya" had ordered his suitcases to be packed...* The young man with a French crop sitting opposite Kuzma flushed, got excited and hastened to intervene:

"Permit me, gentlemen! Here you are saying – liberty… Take me, I work as a clerk for a tax inspector and I send short articles to city newspapers… Is that anything to do with him? He swears he too is for liberty, but at the same time, when he found out that I'd written about the irregular organization of our fire service, he summons me and he says: 'If you write any more of these things, you son of a bitch, I'll unscrew your head!' Pardon me: if my views are to the left of his…"

"Views?" the young man's neighbour suddenly cried in the alto voice of a pygmy – the flour-dealer Chernyayev, a fat castrate* in bottle-shaped boots, who had been looking askance at him all the time with his piggy eyes. And giving him no chance to collect himself, he shrieked:

"Views? Is it you that has views? Is it you that's to the left? I saw you when you were still running around without any trousers on! You were pegging out from hunger, just like your scrounging father! You ought to wash the inspector's feet and drink the water!"

"The con-sti-tu-u-tion," sang Kuzma in a thin voice, interrupting the castrate, and rising from his place, catching the knees of the seated people, he went down the carriage to the doors.

The castrate's legs were small, plump and unpleasant, like some old housekeeper's, and his face was like a woman's as well – large, yellow, chubby, the lips thin… And Polozov was a fine one too, a teacher from the secondary school, the one who had been nodding his head so sweetly while listening to the castrate, leaning on his walking stick, a thickset man in a grey hat and a grey cape, clear-eyed, with a round nose and a luxuriant light-brown beard covering his entire chest… Opening the door onto the platform at the end of the carriage, Kuzma inhaled the cold and fragrant rainy freshness with delight. The rain was droning indistinctly on the awning above the platform, pouring down it in streams, flying off in splashes. The carriages were rocking and rumbling amidst the noise of the rain, the telegraph wires were rising and falling as they floated towards them, and to the sides ran the dense, fresh-green edges of a hazel grove. A motley crew of little boys suddenly leapt out from under the embankment and shouted something all together in ringing voices. Touched, Kuzma smiled, and the whole of his face was covered in little wrinkles. And raising his eyes, on the platform opposite he saw a wandering pilgrim: a kind, exhausted, peasant's face, a grey beard, a wide-brimmed hat, a thick tweed coat tied with a rope, a sack and a tin kettle over his shoulders, working boots on thin legs. And he cried through the rumbling and the noise:

"Back from pilgrimage?"

"From Voronezh," replied the wanderer with charming readiness in a weak cry.

"Are they burning landowners there?"

"They are…"

"Wonderful!"

"Eh?"

"Wonderful, I said!" cried Kuzma.

And turning aside, blinking away the tears of emotion that had welled up, with trembling hands he began rolling a cigarette… But his thoughts again grew muddled. "Does the wanderer represent the people, while the castrate and the teacher don't? Slavery was abolished only forty-five years ago – so how can you call these people to account? Yes, but who's to blame for it? The people themselves!" And again Kuzma's face darkened and began to look pinched.

At the fourth station he got off and hired a cart. The peasant drivers asked for seven roubles at first – it was twelve *versts* to Kazakovo – then five and a half. Finally one said: "If you give me three, I'll take you, or else there's no point in blathering on. Things nowadays aren't what they were…" But he could not maintain the tone and added the customary phrase: "And fodder's dear as well…" And he took him for one and a half. The mud was impassable, the cart small, barely holding together, the wretched horse – big-eared, like a donkey, and feeble. They dragged slowly out of the station yard, and the peasant, sitting on the cart's edge, began to get fidgety, jerking on the rope reins as though he wanted with the whole of his being to help the horse. He had boasted at the station that it "couldn't be held back", and now he was evidently ashamed. But what was worst of all was the man himself. Young, huge, plump, in bast shoes and white puttees, in a short *chekmen*, tied with a rope end, and with an old cap on his straight yellow hair. He smelt of a hut with a stove but no chimney, and of hemp – nothing other than a ploughman of days of yore – had a white, whiskerless face, a swollen throat and a husky voice.

"What's your name?" asked Kuzma.

"I was named Akhvanasy…"

"Akhvanasy!" thought Kuzma testily.

"And what else?" Kuzma asked.

"Menshov… Gee up, anchichrist!"

"The pox, is it?" Kuzma nodded at his throat.

"Why should it be the pox," mumbled Menshov, turning his eyes away. "I drank a lot of cold *kvas*…"

"And does it hurt to swallow?"

"To swallow – no, it doesn't…"

"Well don't talk pointless rubbish, then," said Kuzma sternly. "Better get yourself to hospital quickly. I suppose you're married?"

"I am…"

"Well, you see. And when children start to appear, you'll be giving them all the best possible present."

"As sure as eggs is eggs," agreed Menshov.

And getting fidgety, he began jerking on the reins. "Gee up, gee up… You're right out of hand, anchichrist!" In the end he gave this useless business up and relaxed. He was silent for a long time, then suddenly asked:

"Have they assembled the Duma, merchant, or haven't they?"

"They have."

"And Makarov's alive,* they say – only he gave orders not to tell…"

Kuzma even jerked his shoulders up: the devil knows what's inside these heads here in the steppe! "But what riches!" he thought, sitting in agony, with his knees raised, on the bare bottom of the cart, on a tuft of straw covered with sacking, and examining the street. And what black earth! The mud on the roads was blue and rich, the greenery of the trees, the grasses, the kitchen gardens – dark and dense… But the huts were clay-covered, small, with roofs of dung. Beside the huts were cracked water barrels. The water in them had tadpoles in it, of course… Here was a rich homestead. An old threshing barn on the threshing floor. The farmyard, the gates, the hut – all under the one thatched roof. The hut built of brick in two rows, the piers covered in whitewash with drawings on them: on one, a stick with chevrons going up it – a fir tree – on the other, something like a cockerel; the little windows were edged with whitewash too – in zigzags. "Art!" Kuzma smirked. "The age of the caveman, God help us, the caveman!" Above the doors of an outbuilding there were crosses drawn in charcoal, by the porch was a large gravestone – the grandfather or grandmother had evidently got it ready for when they died... Yes, a rich homestead. But the mud all around was knee-deep, and there was a pig lying on the porch. The little windows were tiny, and in the living quarters there was doubtless darkness, constant overcrowding: a bed on the stove, a loom, the huge stove itself, a tub of slops... And a big family, a lot of children, lambs and calves in the winter... And damp, and such fumes that there's a green mist in there. And the children whimper – and yell when they get a slap round the head; the daughters-in-law abuse one another – "may you be struck by thunder, you slut!" – each wishes the other would "choke on something on Easter Day"; the old mother-in-law is continually throwing oven forks and bowls around, flinging herself upon the daughters-in-law, rolling up the sleeves on her dark, sinewy arms, letting rip with shrill abuse, splashing saliva and curses now at one, now at another... Bad-tempered and sick is the old man too, and everyone is worn out by his lecturing...

Further on they turned onto the common. On the common a fair was being set out. In places the frames of tents were already sticking up, there were piles of wheels and clay crockery; a hastily built clay oven was smoking and there was the smell of fritters; there was the grey of a covered gypsy travelling wagon, and beside its wheels sat chained sheepdogs. Further on, beside the state-owned tavern, stood a tightly packed crowd of peasants, men and women, and cries rang out.

"People are making merry," said Menshov pensively.

"What's the reason for it?" asked Kuzma.

"They're hopeful..."

"What of?"

"It's clear, what of... Of a house sprite!"

"Oo-oop!" cried someone in the crowd to the sound of heavy, muffled stamping:

> No ploughing, no reaping –
> Giving girls a squeezing!

And a short peasant standing at the back of the crowd suddenly threw up his arms. Everything he wore was homely, clean, durable – the bast shoes and the puttees, and the new, sackcloth trousers, and the extremely short, bobtailed, gathered skirt of the *poddyovka* of thick grey cloth. He suddenly stamped his bast shoes softly and deftly, threw up his hands and cried in a tenor voice: "Step aside, let the merchant have a look!" and leaping into the broken circle, he began flapping his trousers frenziedly in front of a tall young fellow who, with his cap tilted back, was twisting his boots about devilishly, and throwing off a black *poddyovka* from over a new cotton shirt as he did so. The fellow's face was focused, gloomy, pale and sweaty.

"My son! My precious!" in the midst of the din and staccato stamping came the wailing of an old woman in a woollen skirt with her arms outstretched. "Stop it, for Christ's sake! My precious, stop – you'll die!"

And her son suddenly threw up his head, clenched his fists and teeth, and with a furious face cried out as he stamped:

Hush, granny, stop your clucking...

"She's sold her last pieces of linen for him as it is," said Menshov, dragging across the common. "She loves him madly – she's a widow woman – but he's drunk and gives her a thrashing practically ev'ry day... She evidently deserves it."

"And how's that – 'deserves it'?" asked Kuzma.

"Don't indulge him – that's how..."

On a bench by one hut sat a lanky peasant – better-looking corpses get put in coffins: his legs stood in his felt boots like sticks, his large, deathly hands lay flat on his sharp knees, on his well-worn trousers. His hat was pulled down low on his forehead, in the style of an old man, his eyes were tormented, imploring, his inhumanly thin face was drawn, his lips ashen and half open...

"That's Craw-deil," said Menshov, nodding at the sick man. "He's been dying for more than a year from his stomach."

"Craw-deil? What's that then – a nickname?"

"A nickername..."

"Stupid!" said Kuzma.

And he turned away so as not to see the little girl beside the next hut: she was leaning backwards, holding a child in a bonnet in her arms, staring fixedly at the people riding by and, sticking out her tongue, was chewing away, preparing a dummy of black bread for the child... And on the final threshing floor the willows were droning in the wind and a crooked scarecrow's empty sleeves were flapping. A threshing floor that

77

looks out onto the steppe is always unwelcoming, miserable, and here there was this scarecrow too, and autumnal rain clouds, because of which there was a bluish tone to everything, and the wind was droning from the fields, fanning the tails of the hens that were wandering about on the threshing floor, overgrown with goosefoot and mugwort, and beside the threshing barn with its gaping roof ridge...

The little wood showing up blue on the horizon – two long hollows overgrown with oak trees – was called Trouse. And by that Trouse Kuzma was caught by torrential rain with hail, which accompanied him all the way to Kazakovo. Menshov drove his wretched horse at a gallop outside the village, and Kuzma sat with his eyes screwed up under wet, cold sacking. His hands grew numb with cold; icy rivulets ran down inside the collar of his *chuika*; the sacking, grown heavy in the rain, stank of a mouldy corn bin. The hailstones struck him on the head, cakes of mud flew, the water sloshed in the ruts beneath the wheels, lambs were bleating somewhere... It finally became so stuffy that Kuzma flung the sacking back off his head. The rain was easing, evening was coming on, a herd was running past the cart and across the green common towards the huts. A thin-legged black sheep had strayed off to one side, and chasing after it was a barefooted woman, covering her head with her wet skirt and with her white calves flashing. In the west, beyond the village, it was getting lighter, and in the east, against the dusty-grey background of a rain cloud, two green and violet arcs stood above the crops. The greenery of the fields smelt dense and moist, the dwellings – warm.

"Where's the master's house hereabouts?" Kuzma shouted to a broad-shouldered peasant woman in a white blouse and red woollen skirt.

The woman was standing on the stone step of a hut and holding a wailing girl by the hand. The girl's wailing was unbelievably piercing.

"House?" the woman repeated. "Whose?"

"The master's."

"Whose? Can't hear a thing... Oh, why don't you choke, or get struck by convulsions!" the woman shouted, jerking the girl by the arm so hard that she toppled over.

They asked at another homestead. They drove down a wide street, veered left, then right, and passing someone's old-world manor with the house tightly boarded up, they started to go steeply downhill towards a bridge over a little river. Drops were falling from Menshov's face, hair and *chekmen*. His rinsed fat face with large white eyelashes seemed even more obtuse. He kept glancing curiously at something up ahead. Kuzma took a look too. On the other side, on sloping common ground, was the dark Kazakovo orchard, a wide yard, enclosed by crumbling outbuildings, and the ruins of a stone wall; in the middle of the yard, behind three dried-up fir trees, was a house faced with grey boards under a rust-red roof. Below, by a bridge, was a knot of peasants. And ahead, struggling in the mud where the steep road had been washed away, pulling itself up and out, was a team of three thin workhorses harnessed to a tarantass. A ragged but handsome farm labourer, pale, with a little reddish beard and intelligent eyes, was standing beside the troika, jerking on the reins, straining himself and crying: "Gee up! Gee up, gee up!" And the peasants were joining in with a cackling and a whistling: "Whoa! Whoa!" And with desperately outstretched arms, a young woman in mourning clothes was sitting in the tarantass with big tears on her long eyelashes. Despair was also in the turquoise eyes of the fat, ginger-whiskered man who was sitting beside her. A wedding ring gleamed on his right hand, which was gripping a revolver; he kept on waving the left one, and he must have been very hot in a camel-hair *poddyovka* and a cloth cap, which had slid down onto the back of his head. And gazing around with meek curiosity from the bench opposite the seat were some children – a boy and a girl, pale, and bundled up in shawls.

"That's Mishka Siversky," said Menshov in a loud, hoarse voice, driving around the troika and looking with indifference at the children. "He was burnt down yesterday… Obviously deserves it…"

The affairs of the masters of Kazakovo were managed by the head-man, a former cavalry soldier, a strapping and coarse man. He was the one that needed to be spoken to, in the servants' hut, as Kuzma was told by a workman driving into the yard in a cart of long, wet, green, mowed grass. The headman had had a misfortune that day – a child had died – and Kuzma was met with an unfriendly greeting. When he went up to the servants' hut, leaving Menshov outside the gate, the tear-stained, serious wife of the headman was coming from the orchard carrying a speckled hen, which sat quietly under her arm. Between the pillars on the ramshackle porch stood a tall young man in long boots and a calico *kosovorotka*, and, on seeing the headman's wife, he cried:

"Agafya, where are you going with that?"

"To kill it," replied the headman's wife, seriously and sadly.

"Let me do it."

And the young man made for the ice house, paying no attention to the rain which had again begun spitting from the frowning sky. Opening the door of the ice house, he picked up an axe from the doorstep – and a moment later a short thud rang out, and a headless chicken with a little red stump of a neck started running about on the grass; it stumbled and began spinning around, fluttering its wings and tossing feathers and flecks of blood in all directions. The young man threw down the axe and made for the orchard, while the headman's wife, after catching the chicken, went up to Kuzma:

"What do you want?"

"It's about the orchard," said Kuzma.

"Wait for Fyodor Ivanych."

"And where is he?"

"He'll be back from the fields soon."

And Kuzma began waiting by the open window of the servants' hut. He glanced inside, and in the semi-darkness saw a stove, a plank bed, a table, a trough on a bench by the window – a coffin in the form of a trough, where there lay the dead child with a large, almost bare head and a little bluish face... At the table sat a fat, blind girl fishing pieces of bread and milk from a bowl with a large wooden spoon. Flies were droning above her like bees in a hive, crawling over the dead face, then falling into the milk, but the blind girl, sitting upright like a stone statue, with her wall eyes staring into the gloom, just kept on eating. Kuzma started to feel terrible, and he turned away. A cold wind was blowing in gusts, and it was getting ever darker because of the rain clouds. In the middle of the yard rose two poles with a crosspiece, and from the crosspiece there hung, like an icon, a large sheet of cast iron: that meant they were afraid in the night, they beat on it. Lying around in the yard were thin borzoi hounds. A boy of about eight was running around amongst them, giving a ride in a handcart to his white-headed, bull-faced little brother in a large black cap – and the cart was squealing furiously. The house was grey and squat, and must have been damnably dreary in this twilight. "They might at least light a light!" thought Kuzma. He was dead tired, it seemed to him that he had driven out of town almost a year before...

But he spent the evening and night in the orchard. Arriving from the fields on horseback, the headman said angrily that "the orchard was letted long ago", and at a request for a place for the night was only insolently amazed: "You're a clever one, though!" he shouted. "It's a nice inn you've found! There's loads of your kind knocking around nowadays…" But he did take pity and allow him to spend the night in the orchard, in the bathhouse. Kuzma settled up with Menshov and went past the house towards the gates of a lime avenue. From the dark, open windows, from behind wire netting to stop the flies, a grand piano was ringing out, drowned by a magnificent voice, by intricate vocal exercises, which were not at all in keeping with either the evening or the manor house. Moving unhurriedly towards Kuzma along the dirty sand of the sloping avenue, at the end of which, as at the edge of the world, there was the dim whiteness of the cloudy sky, was a dark-red-haired little peasant with a bucket in his hand, beltless, without a hat and in heavy boots.

"How about that then, how about that!" he was saying mockingly as he walked, listening intently to the vocal exercises. "How about that, doing just as he likes!"

"Who's doing as he likes?" asked Kuzma.

The little peasant raised his head and paused.

"Why, the young master," he said cheerfully, with a heavy burr. "Been doing it for seven years, they say!"

"And who is he – the one that gave the chicken the chop?"

"N-no, another one… But this is nothing. There are times when he starts crying: 'You today, me tomorrow' – it's downright aw-awful!"

"He's learning, I suppose?"

"Nice learning!"

This was all said seemingly carelessly, in passing, with pauses for breath, but with such a sarcastic grin and burr that Kuzma gave this man he had met an attentive glance. Looks like a simpleton. Long, straight hair in a pudding-basin cut. The face small, insignificant, old Russian, from Suzdal. Enormous boots, a skinny and somehow wooden body. The eyes beneath large, sleepy lids are hawkish, with a golden circle in the pupil. He lowers the lids, and he's an ordinary simpleton, raises them – and it's even a little frightening.

"Do you stay in the orchard?" asked Kuzma.

"In the orchard. Where else?"

"And what's your name?"

"Mine? Akim... And yours?"

"I wanted to rent the orchard."

"So that's it... missed the boat!"

And with a mocking shake of the head, Akim went on his way.

The wind blew ever more gustily, sprinkling splashes from the bright-green trees, and beyond the orchard, somewhere low down, taut thunder was rumbling, flashes of pale-blue lightning lit up the avenue, and everywhere the nightingales were singing. It was quite incomprehensible how they could chatter, trill and spill out their song so diligently, in such a persistent state of oblivion, so sweetly and powerfully under this heavy, leaden, cloudy sky, amidst the trees bending in the wind, in the dense, wet bushes. But even more incomprehensible was how the watchmen spent the night in this wind, how they slept on damp straw under the awning of a mouldy withy hut!

There were three of them. And all were ill. A young former baker, now a vagabond, complained of a fever; another, also a vagabond, but already a chronic one, had consumption, although he said that he was all right, he only got "cold between the wings"; Akim suffered from "night blindness" – because of cachexia he could not see well in the dusk. The baker, pale and friendly, was squatting beside the hut when Kuzma approached, and with the sleeves of his wadded jacket rolled up on his thin, weak arms, he was rinsing millet in a wooden cup. Consumptive Mitrofan, a man short in stature, broad and dark-faced, dressed all in wet rags and down-at-heel shoes, battered and rough, like an old horseshoe, was standing beside the baker, with his shoulders raised, gazing at his work with brown, gleaming eyes, dilated and expressionless. Akim had lugged the bucket here, and was lighting a fire, blowing on the flame in a hollow in the ground opposite the hut. He was going into the hut, choosing the drier wisps of straw that were there and, going back to the fragrantly smoking fire under a cast-iron pot, he was continually muttering something, breathing with a whistling noise and smiling carelessly, with mocking mystery, at the teasing of his partners, and at times cutting them short viciously and cleverly. And Kuzma closed his eyes and listened now to the conversation, now to the nightingales, as he sat on the damp bench beside the hut, besprinkled with icy splashes when the damp wind flew down the avenue beneath the gloomy, rumbling sky, which shuddered at the pale summer lightning.

There was a gnawing in the pit of his stomach caused by hunger and shag tobacco. It seemed as if the skilly would never be ready, and the thought would not leave his head that maybe he too would have to live just such an animal life as these watchmen... And he was irritated by the gusts of wind, the distant, monotonous thunder, the nightingales, and by the leisurely, carelessly sarcastic burr of Akim, and his grating voice.

"You might at least buy a belt, Akimushka," said the baker with feigned naivety, teasing, and throwing glances at Kuzma, inviting him too to listen to Akim.

"Just wait," replied Akim in absent-minded mockery, removing some scum from the pot which had now come to the boil. "We'll live out the summer with the master, and I'll buy you a pair of boots with a right squeak."

"'With a khright squeak'! I'm not asking you to do that."

"And there you are in your down-at-heel shoes."

And Akim began carefully tasting the liquid from the spoon.

The baker was embarrassed and sighed:

"It's not for the likes of us to be wearing boots!"

"Stop it now," said Kuzma, "better, you tell me how you look after yourselves here. I suppose it's skilly and more skilly every day?"

"What, did you fancy some fish or some ham?" asked Akim, without turning round and while licking the spoon. "It wouldn't be bad, that: a nice quarter-pint of vodka, three pounds or so of sheat fish, a little end of ham, some fruit tea... And this isn't skilly, it's called thin porridge."

"And do you cook cabbage soup, broth?"

"We did have some, brother, some cabbage soup, and what soup too! Splash it on a dog and it'd take its coat right off!"

Kuzma shook his head:

"It's because of your illness you're so bad-tempered, isn't it? Perhaps you ought to get some treatment..."

Akim did not answer. The fire was already dying out, underneath the pot a little pile of slender coals was glowing red; the orchard was growing darker and darker, and the light-blue flashes of lightning in the gusts of wind that puffed out Akim's shirt had started to give a pale illumination to their faces. Mitrofan sat leaning on a stick next to Kuzma, the baker sat on a stump underneath a lime tree. On hearing Kuzma's last words, the baker became serious.

83

"Well this is the way I think," he said humbly and sadly, "that it's none other than the Lord all the time. If the Lord doesn't grant you health, then no doctors'll help you. What Akim there says is true: you won't die before your time."

"Doctors!" Akim joined in, gazing at the coals and pronouncing the word with particular sarcasm: dokhtorkhs!... "Doctors, brother, watch over their pockets. I'd let his guts out for him, that doctor, for his work!"

"Not all of them do," said Kuzma.

"I've not seen them all."

"Well don't invent things, then, if you've not seen them," Mitrofan said sternly, and turned to the baker. "And you're a fine one too: hark at you, singing out with your hard-luck stories! If you didn't lie about on the ground like a dog, I don't suppose you'd be writhing around so."

"But I mean, I..." the baker made to begin.

But at this point the mocking calm suddenly left Akim. And opening his hawkish eyes wide, he suddenly leapt up and cried out with the quick temper of an idiot:

"What? You mean I'm the one that shouldn't invent things? Have *you* been in a hospital? Have you? Well, I have! I was in there for seven days – and did he feed me lots of buns, that dokhtor of yours? Did he?"

"You fool," Mitrofan interrupted, "buns aren't supposed to be for everyone: it's according to your illness."

"Ah! According to your illness! Well, may he choke on them, may his belly burst!" cried Akim.

And gazing around furiously, he chucked the spoon into the "thin porridge" and went into the hut.

There, breathing with a whistling noise, he lit the lamp, and inside the hut it grew cosy. Then he got spoons out from somewhere under the roof, threw them onto the table and shouted: "So, bring the skilly, then!" The baker stood up and went to get the pot. "Be our guest," he said, walking past Kuzma. But Kuzma asked only for some bread, salted it well and, chewing with pleasure, went back again to the bench. It had become completely dark. Pale-blue light lit up the rustling trees ever wider, quicker and brighter, as if the wind were blowing on it, and at every flash of lightning, the ghastly-green foliage became visible for a moment as if it were daytime, after which everything was flooded in sepulchral blackness. The nightingales had fallen silent – only one was chattering and spilling its song out sweetly and powerfully, right above the hut. "They've not even asked who I am, where I'm from," thought Kuzma. "The people, the devil take them!" And he cried jokingly into the hut:

"Akim! You've not even asked who I am, where I'm from."

"And what good are you to me?" replied Akim.

"I'm asking him about something else now," came the voice of the baker, "how much land does he hope to get from the Duma? What do you think, Akimushka? Ah?"

"I'm not lit'rate," said Akim. "You know better from out of the dung."

And the baker must have been embarrassed again: for a moment there was silence.

"That's the likes of us he's talking about," began Mitrofan. "I was saying once that in Rostov, the poor people, the proletariat, that is, use dung to survive in the winter..."

"They go out from the town," Akim chimed in gleefully, "and – into the dung! Bury themselves no worse than a pig, and they don't give a hang."

"You fool!" snapped Mitrofan. "What are you cackling for? When poverty catches up with you, you will bury yourself too!"

Lowering his spoon, Akim looked at him sleepily. And with that same, sudden quick temper as a while before, he opened up his empty, hawkish eyes and cried furiously:

"A-ah! Poverty! Did you want work that's paid by the hour?"

"What else then?" Mitrofan cried furiously too, dilating his Dahomeyan nostrils and staring straight at Akim with gleaming eyes. "Twenty hours for a twenty-kopek piece?"

"A-ah! And you'd like a rouble per hour? Terribly greedy, may your belly burst!"

But the argument died down just as quickly as it had flared up. A minute later Mitrofan was already saying calmly, scalding himself with the skilly:

"So he's not the greedy one?! He hangs onto every kopek for dear life, the blind devil. Can you believe it – he sold his wife for fifteen kopeks! Honest to God, I'm not joking. In Lipetsk we've got this little old man, Pankov he's called, and he used to work in the orchards too, well, but now he's retired, and he's very fond of you know what..."

"Akim's from Lipetsk too, then?" asked Kuzma.

"From the village of Studenka," said Akim indifferently, as though the conversation were not even about him.

"He lives with his brother," Mitrofan confirmed. "He owns the land and the homestead jointly with him, only they think of him as a bit of a simpleton all the same, and his wife has already run away from him, of course; and the reason why she ran away – it's precisely because of this here, you know: he made a bargain with Pankov, to let him into the storeroom to take his place in the night for fifteen kopeks – and let him in he did."

Akim was silent, occasionally tapping his spoon on the table and gazing at the lamp. He had already had enough to eat, had wiped himself, and was now thinking about something.

"Talking's one thing, fellow, and doing is another," he said finally. "And even if I did let him in: did it do her any harm?"

And listening intently, he grinned, raised his eyebrows, and his Suzdal face became joyfully sad and was covered in big, wooden wrinkles.

"I wish I could let him have it with a rifle!" he said, with the grating voice and the burr particularly marked. "He'd turn head over heels so nicely."

"Who's that you're talking about?" asked Kuzma.

"That there nightingale…"

Kuzma gritted his teeth and, after some thought, said:

"You're a stinker of a man. An animal."

"Kiss my arse," responded Akim. And with a hiccup, he rose:

"Well, why burn the light for no khreason?"

Mitrofan started to roll a cigarette, the baker to clear away the spoons, while Akim climbed out from the table, turned his back to the lamp and, crossing himself hastily three times, made a low bow towards a dark corner of the hut, gave his wiry, straight hair a shake and, lifting his face, began whispering a prayer. He cast a big, fractured shadow onto some wooden crates of some sort. He crossed himself hurriedly again and again, made a low bow – and already Kuzma glanced at him with hatred. Here was Akim praying – and just try asking him whether he believed in God! His hawkish eyes would jump out of their sockets! What, was he some sort of Tatar?

It seemed as if he had driven out of town a year before, and he would never get back to it now. His wet cap was a burden, his cold feet ached, cramped inside his muddy boots. His face had been lashed by the wind during the day and it was burning. Rising from the bench, Kuzma set off against the damp wind towards the gate into the fields, towards the wasteland of a long-disused churchyard. A weak light from the hut fell onto the mud, but, as soon as Kuzma moved away, Akim blew on the lamp, the light disappeared and immediately night fell. Bluish lightning flashed more boldly, more unexpectedly, revealing the entire sky, the entire depths of the orchard as far as the distant fir trees where the bathhouse stood, then suddenly flooded everything in such blackness that his head started spinning. And again, somewhere low down, there was a rumble of distant thunder. After standing for a while and distinguishing a dim shaft of light in a gateway, Kuzma went out onto the road which ran by the bank, by the rustling old limes and maples, and began walking slowly backwards and forwards. Rain sprinkled again onto his cap, onto his hands. And again the black darkness was thrown open to its depths, the drops of rain began to sparkle, and outlined on the wasteland, in the deathly blue light, was the figure of a wet, slender-necked horse. There was a glimpse against the inky background of a pale, metallic-green field of oats beyond the wasteland, but the horse raised its head – and Kuzma felt frightened. He turned back towards the gate. And when he had groped his way to the bathhouse standing in the fir grove, the rain came down onto the earth with such force that, as in childhood, terrible thoughts started flashing through his mind of a flood. He struck a match, saw a wide plank bed beside the window and, rolling up his jacket, he tossed it to the bedhead. In the darkness he climbed onto the bed and with a deep sigh stretched out upon it, lay down on his back like an old man and closed his tired eyes. My God, what an absurd and difficult journey! And how had he ended up here? In the masters' house there was also darkness now, and the flashes of lightning were reflected in passing, stealthily, in the mirrors... In the hut, in torrential rain, Akim was asleep... In this here bathhouse, of course, devils had been seen many a time: did Akim believe properly in the Devil at least? No. But he told with certainty all the same of how his late grandfather – it would have to be his grandfather and he would have to be dead – had once gone into a threshing barn for some haulm, and the Devil had just been sitting there on a rein with his legs crossed, as shaggy as a dog... And raising one knee, Kuzma put his wrist on his forehead and, sighing and depressed, started to doze off...

He spent the summer waiting for a job. Dreams of orchards proved very silly. Returning to town and having a good think about his situation, he began looking for a job as a shop assistant, a clerk; then he started agreeing to anything – as long as there was a crust of bread. But searches, efforts, requests went to waste. And he was gripped by despair: how had he failed to see there was no point in his even hoping! He had been thought of in town as a great eccentric for a long, long time. Drunkenness and idleness turned him into a laughing stock. His life at first astonished the town, then began to seem suspicious. And rightly so: it was unheard of for a townsman of his age to be living in a hostel, to be a bachelor and as beggarly as an organ-grinder: all his property was a small trunk and a heavy old umbrella! And Kuzma started having a look in the mirror: indeed, what sort of a man was it before him? He spends the night in a "dormitory" among strangers, people who come and go, in the morning he trudges through the heat to the market, to the taverns, where he tries to pick up rumours of jobs; he sleeps in the afternoon, then sits by a window and reads, gazes at the dusty white street and the sky, pale-blue from the heat… For whom and for what is this man alive in the world, thin, already grey-haired from hunger and stern thoughts, calling himself an anarchist and not really knowing how to explain what the word means? He sits and reads; he'll sigh, take a turn around the room; he'll squat down, unlock his trunk; he'll rearrange more neatly the tatty books and manuscripts, the two or three faded *kosovorotkas*, the old, long-skirted frock coat, the waistcoat, the worn birth certificate… And what is he to do next?

And the summer dragged on for an endlessly long time. There was now a hellish dry spell in town. The corner building of the hostel roasted in the sun. In the night the stuffy heat would make the blood pulse into your head, and every sound outside the open windows would wake you up. But it was impossible to sleep in the hayloft because of the fleas, the crying of the cockerels and the stench of the dung yard. All summer long, the dream of visiting Voronezh never abandoned Kuzma. Of at least wandering about the Voronezh streets between one train and the next, looking at the familiar poplars and that little blue house outside the town… But what was the point? To spend ten or fifteen roubles and then deny himself a candle, a bun? And it was shameful for an old man to give himself up to amorous recollections. And as for Klasha, well, was she even his daughter? He had seen her a couple of years before:

sitting at the window making lace, sweet and modest in appearance, but resembling only her mother...

By autumn Kuzma was convinced that it was essential either to go away and visit holy places, to go to some monastery or other, or – simply to jerk a razor across his throat. Autumn was approaching. The market already smelt of apples and plums. The grammar-school boys had arrived. The sun began setting behind Schepnaya Square: you would go out of the gates in the evening and, going across the crossroads, you would be blinded: the whole street to the left, running into the square in the distance, was flooded in a low, dreary light. The gardens behind the fences were covered in dust and cobwebs. Polozov would be coming towards you wearing a loose cloak, but his soft hat had already been replaced by a cap with a cockade. In the town gardens there wasn't a soul. The bandstand was boarded up, the kiosk where in the summer they sold fermented mare's milk and lemonade was boarded up, the wooden snack bar was closed. And one day, sitting beside the bandstand, Kuzma got so depressed that now he fell into serious thought about suicide. The sun was setting, its light was reddish, small pink leaves were flying down the tree-lined avenue, a cold wind was blowing. At the cathedral they were ringing for vespers, and to this rhythmical, dense sound of the ringing, the sound of the provinces, of a Saturday, his soul ached unbearably. Suddenly, from inside the bandstand, there came a coughing, a groaning... "Motka," thought Kuzma. And it was: out from under the steps clambered Motya Duckhead. He was wearing ginger-coloured soldier's boots, an extremely long grammar-school uniform jacket bestrewn with flour – the market had evidently had a bit of fun – and a straw hat which had many a time gone under wheels. Without opening his eyes, spitting and swaying from a hangover, he went past. Holding back tears, Kuzma himself called to him:

"Motya! Come and have a chat and a smoke..."

And Motya came back, sat down on the bench and, with shifting brows, began sleepily rolling a cigarette, but he seemed unable to grasp properly who it was next to him, who it was complaining to him about his fate...

And the next day that same Motya brought Tikhon's note to Kuzma.

At the end of September Kuzma moved to Durnovka.

3

I N THAT DISTANT TIME when Ilya Mironov had lived for a couple of years in Durnovka, Kuzma had been no more than a child, and there remained in his memory only the dark-green, fragrant hemp fields in which Durnovka was awash, as well as one dark summer's night: there had been not a single light in the village, but past Ilya's hut, with their blouses white in the darkness, had gone "nine maidens, nine wives and a tenth a widow", all barefooted, bare-headed, with brooms, clubs and pitchforks, and there had been a deafening ringing and banging on stove doors and frying pans, which had itself been drowned out by a wild choral song: the widow had been dragging a plough along, next to her had walked a maiden with a large icon, and the others had been ringing and banging, and, when the widow had led off in a low voice:

> Don't you, cow's death,
> Come into our village!

the choir had sung the second part in the long-drawn-out tones of a dirge:

> We are ploughing around

and mournfully, in sharp, throaty voices, had carried on:

> With incense and a cross...

Now the look of the Durnovka fields was humdrum. On his way from Vorgol, Kuzma was cheerful and slightly tipsy – Tikhon Ilyich had treated him to fruit liqueur at dinner and been very kind that day – and looked with pleasure at the flat expanses of dry, brown ploughed fields spread out around him. The almost summery sun, the transparent air, the clear, pale-blue sky – everything gladdened him and promised long-term rest. There was so much grey-headed, gnarled wormwood, turned over and uprooted by ploughs, that it was being carried away by the cartload. In a ploughed field right by the estate stood a wretched horse with burrs on its withers and a cart loaded high with wormwood, while next to it lay Yakov, barefooted, in short, dust-coated trousers and a long hempen shirt, keeping down a large, grey-haired dog with his side and holding it by the ears. The dog was growling and looking askance.

"Does it bite?" shouted Kuzma.

"It's vicious – and I've had enough of it!" Yakov responded hurriedly, lifting his crooked beard. "It jumps up at the horses' faces…"

And Kuzma laughed with pleasure. This really was a proper peasant, this was the proper steppe!

But the road was going gently down the hillside and the horizon was narrowing. Ahead was the new green roof of the threshing barn, which seemed to have drowned in the wild, stunted orchard. Beyond the orchard, on the opposite hillside, stood a long row of huts made of mud bricks under straw roofs. To the right, beyond ploughed fields, stretched a large gully, which ran into the one that separated the estate from the village. And on the ridge where the gullies met, there protruded the sails of two open windmills, surrounded by several peasant smallholders' huts – the Ridgemen's, as Oska called them – and showing up white on the common was the whitewashed school.

"So, do the kids have lessons?" asked Kuzma.

"Certainly," said Oska. "Their learner's a daredevil!"

"How's that – learner? Teacher, do you mean?"

"Well, teacher, same thing. He's got that lot schooled, I'm telling you, good as can be. A soldier. Beats them mercilessly, but then he's got everything sorted out! I dropped in once with Tikhon Ilyich – the way they all leapt up at once and barked out: 'Good day, sir!' – you aren't even going to find soldiers like that!"

And again Kuzma laughed.

And when they had driven past the threshing floor, rolled down the muddy road past the cherry orchard and turned left into a long yard, dried out and glistening in the sun, his heart even began to thump: here he was, home at last. And going up onto the porch, stepping over the threshold, Kuzma bowed low to the dark icon in the corner of the entrance hall…

Opposite the house, with their backs towards Durnovka and the broad gully, there stood the barns. From the porch of the house Durnovka could be seen a little to the left, and to the right, a part of the ridge: a windmill and the school. The rooms were small and empty. Rye had been poured into the study, in the reception hall and drawing room there were just a few chairs with torn seats. The drawing-room windows looked out onto the orchard, and for the whole of the autumn Kuzma spent the nights there without ever closing the windows. The floor was never swept: a widow nicknamed Smallholder, the former lover of the young Durnovo, lived in to begin with as cook, and she had to run off to see her little children and cook something for the family, as well as for Kuzma and the workman. Kuzma got the samovar going himself in the mornings, and then he sat by the window in the reception hall having tea with apples. In the morning lustre, beyond the gully, the village roofs gave off a dense smoke. The orchard smelt freshly sweet. And at midday the sun was over the village, it was hot in the yard, and the maples and limes in the orchard glowed, quietly dropping their multicoloured leaves. Doves, warmed by the sun, slept all day on the slope of the kitchen roof, which was yellow with new straw in the clear blue sky. The workman rested after dinner. Smallholder went home. And Kuzma wandered. He walked to the threshing floor, glad of the sunshine, the firm road, the tall, dry weeds, the mangels, which had now turned brown, the nice late flower of the blue chicory and the down of the burdock flying quietly through the air. The ploughed fields gleamed in the sun with the silky networks of cobwebs that covered them over a boundless area. Goldfinches sat dotted about the allotments on dry burdock. On the threshing floor, in the profound quietness, in full sun, grasshoppers chirred ardently... Kuzma climbed over the bank from the threshing floor and returned to the manor house through the orchard and the fir wood. In the orchard he chatted with the townsfolk who were renting it, and with Bride and Nanny-goat, who were gathering windfalls, and climbed with them into the midst of the overgrown nettles where the very ripest lay. Sometimes he ambled into the village, to the school...

The soldier-turned-teacher, stupid by nature, had lost absolutely all sense when in the army. In appearance he was the most ordinary peasant. But he always spoke so extraordinarily and came out with such nonsense that all you could do was spread your arms in bewilderment. He was forever smiling at something or other with the greatest slyness, he gazed at his interlocutor condescendingly, narrowing his eyes, and never answered questions straight away.

"What are you called?" Kuzma asked him, dropping into the school for the first time.

The soldier narrowed his eyes and had a think.

"Without a name, even a sheep's a ram," he said at last unhurriedly. "But I'll ask you a question too: Adam – is that a name or isn't it?"

"It is."

"Right. And how many people, for instance, have died since his time?"

"I don't know," said Kuzma. "But what are you getting at?"

"Because the thing is, that's something we'll never understand. For instance, I'm a soldier and a farrier. I'm walking through the fair not long ago, and what do you know, there's a horse with glanders. I go to the district police officer at once: it's like this, Your Honour. 'And can you kill the horse with a feather?' – 'With great pleasure!'"

"What feather?" asked Kuzma.

"A goose feather. I got one, sharpened it, stuck it in the main vein, blew into the feather a little – and that was that. A simple matter, you'd think, but just you try doing it!"

And the soldier gave a sly wink and tapped a finger on his forehead:

"There's mother wit here as well!"

Kuzma shrugged his shoulders and fell silent. And only when he was passing by Smallholder's did he learn from her Senka what the soldier's name was. Parmen, it turned out.

"And what have you been given to do for tomorrow?" added Kuzma, gazing curiously at Senka's fiery forelocks, at his lively green eyes, freckled face, puny little body, and hands and feet cracked by dirt and a rash.

"Sums, a poem," said Senka, grabbing the foot he had lifted up behind him with his right hand and hopping on the spot.

"What sums?"

"Counting geese. A flock of geese was flying…"

"Oh, I know," said Kuzma. "And what else?"

"Mice as well…"

"Counting them too?"

"Yes. There were six mice carrying six half-kopeks each," Senka mumbled quickly, looking sidelong at Kuzma's silver watch chain. "One mouse who was skinnier was carrying two half-kopeks… How much does it all come to…"

"Tremendous. And what poem?"

Senka let go of his foot.

"The poem 'Who is He?'."*

"Have you learnt it?"

"Yes…"

"Go on then."

And Senka mumbled even quicker about a horseman riding through the forests above the Neva where there were only

The fir, the pine and grey-aired moss…

"Grey-haired," said Kuzma, "not aired."

"All right, eared," agreed Senka.

"And who's this horseman then?"

Senka had a think.

"He's a wizard," he said.

"Right. Well, tell your mother she should at least cut your hair at the front. It's worse for you, isn't it, when the teacher gives it a tug."

"But then he'll find m'years," said Senka carelessly, taking hold of his foot again, and he set off hopping across the common.

The Ridge and Durnovka, as is always the way with adjacent villages, lived in constant hostility and mutual contempt. The Ridgemen considered the people of Durnovka robbers and beggars, as the people of Durnovka did the Ridgemen. Durnovka belonged to "the master", while on the Ridge there dwelt "freemen", smallholders. Only Smallholder was outside the hostility, outside the feuds. Small, thin and neat, she was lively, equable and pleasant in manner and observant. She knew every family both on the Ridge and in Durnovka as well as she did her own, and was the first to inform the manor house of every village occurrence, even the slightest. And everyone knew her life very well too. She never concealed anything from anyone, and talked calmly and simply about her husband and about Durnovo.

"What can you do," she said with a little sigh. "The poverty was dreadful, and there wasn't enough grain in the spring. It's got to be said, my man did love me, but you have to resign yourself, you know. The master gave three whole wagons of rye for me. 'What's to be done?' says I to my man. 'Go, of course,' he says. He drove to fetch the rye, drags it off measure by measure, but even he has the tears going drip-drip, drip-drip..."

She worked tirelessly in the daytime; in the night she darned, sewed, and stole screens from the railway. Once, late in the evening, Kuzma drove out to see Tikhon Ilyich, went up the hillside and froze in fear: above the ploughed fields, drowning in the gloom, against the barely glowing strip of sunset, something black and immense was growing and rushing smoothly towards him...

"Who is it?" he cried feebly, pulling on the reins.

"Oh!" the thing that had been growing so quickly and smoothly in the sky cried feebly, in horror, too, and with a crack it fell to pieces.

Kuzma came to his senses, and in the darkness immediately recognized Smallholder. It was she that had been running towards him on her light, bare feet, bent over, with two *sazhen*-high screens* loaded on her back, the kind they put up along the railway in winter to prevent snowdrifts. And she, recovering herself, began to whisper with a quiet laugh:

"You scared me to death. You're running like that in the night and trembling all over, but what can you do? They heat the whole village, it's the only way we can survive..."

Whereas the workman, Purse, was an utterly uninteresting man. There was nothing to talk to him about, and he wasn't talkative anyway. Like the majority of the people of Durnovka, he just kept on repeating old, simple sayings, confirming what had been known for a long, long time. If the weather was getting worse, he would throw looks at the sky:

"The weather's getting worse. A spot of rain's the first thing now for the greeneries."

If fallow was being ploughed a second time, he would remark:

"If you don't re-plough, you'll be left without grain. That's what the old men used to say."

He had been in the army in his time and had been to the Caucasus, but soldiering had left no marks on him. He could not tell you anything about the Caucasus except only that there was mountain upon mountain there, and that terribly hot and strange waters gushed out of the earth there: "You put some lamb in, and it'd be cooked in a minute, and if you didn't take it out in time, it'd be raw again..." And he was not at all proud of having seen the world; he was even contemptuous of people with experience: after all, people only "roam" against their will or through poverty. He did not believe a single rumour – "they're all lying!" – but he did believe, swore to it, that near Basovo recently there had been a cartwheel rolling along in the dusk – a witch – and one of the peasants, being nobody's fool, had gone and caught this wheel, poked the rope from around his waist through the hole and tied the ends together.

"Well, and what then?" asked Kuzma.

"What do you think?" replied Purse. "The witch woke up early on, and lo and behold, she's got the rope sticking out of her mouth and her backside, and the ends tied together on her belly…"

"So why didn't she untie it?"

"The knot must have had the sign of the cross made over it."

"And aren't you ashamed of believing such nonsense?"

"And why should I feel ashamed? People lie, and so do I."

And Kuzma only liked listening to his tunes. You sit in the darkness by the open window, not a light anywhere, just the village black beyond the gully, it's so quiet that the wild apples can be heard falling from the tree around the corner of the house, and he strolls slowly about the yard with a rattle, crooning away dolefully and peacefully in a falsetto voice: "Quiet, you little canary bird…" He kept watch over the estate until morning, and slept in the daytime – there was hardly anything to do: Tikhon Ilyich had made haste to deal with matters at Durnovka early in the year, and of the livestock had left only a horse and a cow.

Clear days were succeeded by cold, bluish-grey, soundless ones. Goldfinches and tomtits began to whistle softly in the bare orchard, crossbills to trill in the fir trees, waxwings and bullfinches appeared, as well as some unhurried, tiny little birds which flew in little flocks from place to place on the threshing floor, where bright-green cereal shoots had already sprouted through the boards laid beneath the stacks; sometimes a silent, light little bird of the same kind would sit in solitude on a blade of grass somewhere in the fields… In the allotments beyond Durnovka they were finishing digging up the last potatoes. Occasionally, towards evening, one of the peasants would stand there for a long time, lost in thought and contemplation of the fields, holding a wicker basket full of ears of grain over his shoulders. It had started to get dark early, and on the estate they said: "How late the engine is passing now!" although the train timetable had not changed

97

in the least... Kuzma sat by the window reading the newspapers all day long; he jotted down his journey to Kazakovo in the spring and the conversations with Akim, he made notes in the old accounts book of what he saw and heard in the village... More than in anyone else, he was interested in Grey.

Grey was the most beggarly and idle peasant in all the village. He leased his land out and did not stay at workplaces. He sat at home, cold and hungry, but thought only about how he could get the tobacco to have a smoke. He was at every gathering, he did not miss a single wedding, a single christening, a single funeral. A drink to seal a deal was never had without him: he poked his nose not only into all the communal village deals, but into all those between neighbours too – after a purchase, a sale, an exchange. Grey's appearance justified his nickname: grey, thin, of medium height, drooping shoulders, a short, ragged, soiled sheepskin jacket, his felt boots falling apart and soled with string, and the less said of his hat, the better. Sitting in his hut, never taking the hat off, not letting his pipe out of his mouth, he had the sort of look that suggested he was forever waiting for something. But in his view he was devilishly unlucky. No proper work came his way, and that was that! And well, he wasn't one to go in for playing at spillikins. Of course, everyone tried to run him down...

"But tongues are always wagging, aren't they," Grey would say. "Put the job in my hands first, and then you can talk."

He had a respectable amount of land – three *desyatins*. But he found himself with taxes to pay for ten people. And Grey was turned off working the land: "You've got no choice but to lease the land out: she needs to be kept in order, mother earth, and what order is there here?" He himself sowed no more than half a field of crops, but even that he would sell with the crops still standing – "getting rid of something good for something bad". And again, he had his reason: just try waiting till it's ready! "It's still better to wait, for instance..." Yakov would mutter, looking to one side and grinning maliciously. But Grey would be grinning too – sadly and scornfully.

"Better!" he smirked. "It's all right for you to talk: you've given the lass away, married the lad off. Whereas look – I've got a whole corner full of kids. They're nobody else's, you know. I keep the nanny goat there for them, I'm fattening up a piglet... They want food and drink too, don't they?"

"Well the goat, for instance, isn't to blame for it all," retorted Yakov, becoming irritated. "We're the ones, for instance, who can think of nothing but vodka and a pipe... a pipe and vodka..."

And to avoid falling out pointlessly with a neighbour, he would hurry to walk away from Grey. But Grey would remark calmly and pointedly in his wake:

"A drunkard, brother, will sleep it off, but a fool never will."

After dividing the family's land with his brother, Grey spent a long time roaming from one abode to another, and hired himself out both in town and on estates. He worked in clover-processing too. And it was while working on the clover that he once got lucky. The artel* which Grey had joined was hired to process a big consignment at eighty kopeks a *pood*,* but the clover went and produced more than two *poods*. They winnowed it, and Grey took on the job of beating the sacks. He filled some bags with grain and bought them. And he got rich: that same autumn he put up a brick hut. But he miscalculated: it turned out that the hut needed heating. And what with, was the question. And he had nothing to feed himself on either. And the top of the hut had to be burnt, and it stood without a roof for a year and went all black. And the chimney went on a horse's collar. True, he didn't yet have the horse, but then you do have to start setting yourself up in life sometime, after all... And Grey gave it up as a bad job: he decided to sell the hut and put up or buy a cheaper, mud-brick one. He reasoned like this: in the hut there would be – well, in the worst case, ten thousand bricks, for a thousand they give five, or even six roubles; so it comes to more than fifty... But there turned out to be three and a half thousand bricks, for the tie beam he had to take not five roubles, but two fifty... Looking anxiously for a new hut for himself, he spent a whole year bargaining only for ones that he could not afford at all. And he reconciled himself to the one he had only in the firm hope of a solid, spacious, warm one in the future.

"I'm not long for this one, I'm telling you straight!" he snapped one day.

Yakov looked at him carefully and shook his hat.

"Right. So you're waiting for your ships to come in, then?"

"And they will," Grey answered mysteriously.

"Oh, give up your foolishness," said Yakov, "get yourself taken on wherever you can, and hold on to the job, for instance, with your teeth..."

But the idea of a good homestead, of order, of some kind of decent, real work was poisoning Grey's whole life. He was miserable being a hired hand.

"That work of yours, it isn't all milk and honey, evidently," said the neighbours.

"It probably would be if you got a master with a bit of sense!"

And suddenly coming to life, Grey would take his cold pipe out of his mouth and start his favourite story: how, when he was a bachelor, he had lived for two whole years in a good and honest way at a priest's near Yelets.

"I could go there even now, and he'd snatch at me with both hands," he exclaimed. "I'd just have to say the word: I've, like, come, Father, to work for you."

"Well, you should go then, for instance…"

"I should go! And that lot there – look at them – a whole cornerful! Of course: another man's misfortune's no trouble of yours… But here's a man perishing senselessly…"

Grey had been perishing senselessly this year too. He sat at home all winter looking anxious, without a fire, cold and hungry; at Lent he somehow managed to fix himself up with the Rusanovs near Tula: in his own area he was no longer taken on. But not a month had gone by before he was utterly sick and tired of the Rusanovs' estate.

"Oh, my lad!" said the steward once. "I can see right through you: you're planning to take to your heels. You sons of bitches collect the money in advance, and then you run for cover."

"Maybe some tramp might do that, but not us," snapped Grey.

But the steward didn't get what he was hinting at. And he had to act more decisively. Once, towards evening, Grey was made to take the haulm for the livestock. He drove to the barn and started stacking the wagon up with straw. The steward came over:

"Didn't I tell you in Russian – to load up with haulm?"

"It's not the right time to be loading that," Grey replied firmly.

"Why's that?"

"Sensible masters give them haulm at dinner time, and not before bed."

"And what sort of a teacher are you?"

"I don't like doing for the animals. That's all there is to this teacher."

"And you're taking them straw?"

"You need to know the right time for everything."

"Stop loading this minute!"

Grey turned pale.

"No, I won't stop working. I mustn't stop working."

"Give the pitchfork here, you dog, and step away before there's trouble."

"I'm not a dog, but a Khristian man. I'll take this load away, and then I'll step away. And I'll go away for good."

"That's unlikely, brother! You'll go away, but you'll be back again in no time, you'll end up in the district court."

Grey leapt down from the wagon and threw the pitchfork into the straw:

"Is that me'll end up there?"

"You!"

"Oh, lad, make sure it's not you ends up there! Perhaps we know something about you too. The master won't be thanking you either, brother…"

Blood rushed to the steward's fat cheeks, which turned purple, and the whites of his eyes goggled:

"Aha! So that's it! Won't be thanking me? Speak up, then, if that's the way things are – why not?"

"I've got nothing to say," Grey mumbled, feeling his legs had grown heavy with fear at once.

"No, brother, you're wrong – you will say!"

"So where did the flour get to?" Grey suddenly cried.

"The flour? What flour's that? What flour?"

"You know what. From the mill…"

With a grip of iron, the steward grabbed Grey by the collar, by the shirt front – and for an instant they both froze.

"What are you doing – grabbing me by the buttons?" Grey asked calmly. "Do you want to strangle me?"

And all of a sudden he shrieked furiously:

"Well, hit me, hit me, while your blood's up!"

And with a jerk he tore himself free and grabbed the pitchfork.

"Lads!" the steward yelled, though there was no one about. "Fetch the headman! Listen: he's tried to stab me, the son of a bitch!"

"Don't try mixing it, or you'll get your nose broken," said Grey, holding the pitchfork a-tilt. "I reckon the times aren't what they were!"

But at this point the steward took a swing at him, and Grey flew head first into the straw...

All summer Grey sat at home again, waiting for bounty from the Duma. All autumn he roamed from homestead to homestead, hoping to latch onto somebody who was going to work on the clover... One day, a new haystack on the edge of the village caught fire. Grey was the first to get to the fire, and he yelled until he was hoarse, scorched his eyelashes, got soaking wet directing the water barrels and the men who threw themselves into the huge, pinkish-gold flame with pitchforks to drag the burning hanks in all directions, and those who simply rushed about amidst the heat, the crackling, the pouring water, the din, the icons, the tubs, the spinning wheels, the rugs piled up beside the huts, the sobbing women, and the black leaves sprinkling down from the charred willows... Sometime in October, when, after torrential rains and an icy storm, the pond froze, and the neighbours' hog slipped down off a frozen knoll, broke through the ice and started to drown, Grey was the first to dash at full tilt into the water to try and save it... The hog drowned all the same, but this gave Grey the right to run from the pond to the servants' hut to demand vodka, tobacco and something to eat. At first he was all purple, his teeth were chattering, and he could barely move his white lips as he changed all his clothes for someone else's, Purse's. Then he revived, got tipsy, began boasting – and told again of how he had worked in a good and honest way for a priest and how cunningly he had married off his daughter a few years before. He sat at the table, chewing greedily, swallowing slices of raw ham, and recounted with self-satisfaction:

"So. She'd got herself involved, Matryushka, that is, with this Yegorka... Well, so she'd got herself involved. So be it. And there am I sitting by the window in the evening, and I see Yegorka's gone past the hut once, twice... and my girl's forever nipping over to the window... So, they've got something brewing, I thinks to myself. And I says to the wife: you feed the animals here, and I'll be off – they've called a village assembly. I sat myself down in the straw behind the hut, and I sit and wait. And the first snow's already fallen. And I see Yegorka sneaking up again from down the road... And here she comes too. They went round behind the cellar, then darted into the new, empty hut alongside. I waited for a bit..."

"What a story!" said Kuzma, and gave a painful grin.

But Grey took this for praise, admiration for his intelligence and cunning. And he continued, now raising his voice, now lowering it caustically:

"Hang on, listen to what happens next. I waited, I'm saying, for a bit – then I'm after them… Leapt up into the doorway – and caught him right on top of her! They got a fright, an awful one. He collapsed onto the ground like a sack – ready for the slaughter – and she was horror-stricken, lying there like a duck… 'Well,' he says, 'kill me now.' That's him. 'I don't nee-eed,' I says, 'for to kill you…' I took his *poddyovka*, his jacket too, and left him in just his drawers – near enough in his birthday suit… 'Well,' I says, 'you can go wherever you like now…' And I went home. And I look, and he's walking along behind me: the snow's white – and he's white too, walking along and wheezing… He's got nowhere to go – where can you turn to? And my Matryona Mikolavna, as soon as I was out of the hut, she was into the fields! Off she went – a neighbour just about managed to catch her by the sleeve right near Basovo and brought her back to me. I let her have a rest and then I says: 'Are we poor or are we not?' She's silent. 'Is your mother a poor wretch or is she sane?' She's silent again. 'How you've embarrassed us, eh? What, going to dump a whole cornerful of them on me are you, little bastards, and I just bat my eyelids? With poverty like ours, you ought to be keeping watch around yourself, not having fun and waving your plait about, you scum!' Well, and I started whacking her – I had this little knout there, well-used… Well, to put it simply, I lashed the whole of her back to shreds until she's writhing at my feet, kissing my boots, and he's sitting wailing on the bench. I set about him, the little darling, later on…"

"And made him marry her?" asked Kuzma.

"That's right!" Grey exclaimed, and sensing that the drink was getting the better of him, he started scraping pieces of ham from his plate and stuffing them into his trouser pockets. "And what a wedding it was too! I wouldn't spare any expense, brother…"

"Well, what a story!" thought Kuzma for a long time after that evening. But the weather was deteriorating. He did not feel like writing, and his melancholy intensified. His only pleasure was when somebody appeared with a request. Barebrow, a completely bald peasant in a huge hat, came several times from Basovo to write a petition against his daughter-in-law's father, who had broken Barebrow's collarbone.

The widow Little Bottle came from the Ridge, all in rags, all wet and icy from the rain, to write letters to her son. She would start to dictate – and then burst into tears.

"The town of Serpukhov, at the Nobles' Baths, Zheltukhin's house…"

And she would start to cry.

"Well?" Kuzma asks, slanting his eyebrows mournfully and gazing at Little Bottle like an old man, over the top of his pince-nez. "Well, I've written that. What next?"

"Next?" asks Little Bottle in a whisper and, trying to get her voice under control, continues:

"Next, m'darling, write nice and proper… To be given, then, to Mikhal Nazarych Khlusov… in person…"

And continues – at times with pauses, at times with no pauses at all:

"A letter to our sweet and dear son Misha, how is it, Misha, you've forgotten us, there's no word from you at all… You know for yourself we're renting, and now they're chasing us out, wherever are we to go now… Misha, our dear son, we beg you for the Lord God's sake to come home as quick as you can…"

And again through tears in a whisper:

"With you here, we can dig out a mud hut, and at least we'll have a place to call our own…"

Storms and icy torrential rains, days like dusk, the mud on the estate besprinkled with the little yellow leaves of the acacias, the boundless ploughed fields and winter crops around Durnovka, and dark clouds moving endlessly above them tormented him again with hatred for this accursed country, where there were snowstorms for eight months and rains for four, and where to answer a call of nature you have to go into the farmyard or the cherry orchard. When the bad weather set in, he had to board the drawing room up tight and move into the reception hall to sleep there all the rest of the winter – as well as dining, and smoking, and spending the long evenings with a dim lamp from the kitchen, pacing from corner to corner in a cap and *chuika*, which barely protected him from the cold and the wind that blew in through the crevices. They sometimes proved to have forgotten to stock up with paraffin, and Kuzma spent the hours of dusk without a light, and in the evening lit a candle end just to have his supper of potato broth and warm millet porridge, served in silence, with a stern face, by Bride.

"Where could I go?" he sometimes thought.

There were only three neighbours nearby: old Princess Shakhova, who did not receive even the Marshal of the Nobility, considering him ill-bred; the retired gendarme Zakrzhevsky, a haemorrhoidally bad-tempered man, who would not allow him even onto his doorstep; and finally the owner of a small estate, Basov, who lived in a hut, had married a simple, widowed peasant woman, and talked only about horse collars and livestock. Father Pyotr, the priest from Kolodezi, which was Durnovka's parish, visited Kuzma once, but neither the one nor the other had any desire to keep up the acquaintance. Kuzma only offered the priest tea, and the priest burst into abrupt and awkward laughter when he saw the samovar on the table. "The samovar? Excellent! I can see you're not lavish with your hospitality!" Kuzma declared candidly that he never went to church because of his convictions – and the priest burst into even more astonished, even more abrupt and louder laughter: "Aha! New ideas? Excellent! It's cheaper that way too!" And the laughter did not suit him at all: it was as though somebody else were laughing on behalf of this tall, thin man with big shoulder blades and thick, black hair and darting eyes. "But before you go to bed, before you go to bed, I expect you cross yourself all the same, get cold feet?" he said loudly and rapidly while putting his coat on in the hallway, and suddenly adopting an intimate tone. "I do," Kuzma confessed with a sad smile. "But fear isn't belief, is it?"

Kuzma was not often at his brother's either. And the latter came only when he was upset about something. And the loneliness was so desperate that at times Kuzma called himself Dreyfus on Devil's Island.* He compared himself with Grey as well. Ah, like Grey, after all, he too was beggarly, weak-willed, and had been waiting all his life for some lucky days for work!

With the first snow, Grey went off somewhere and was away for about a week. He came home gloomy.

"Been to Rusanov's again, have you?" asked the neighbours.

"I have," Grey replied.

"What for?"

"They tried to persuade me to be taken on."

"Right. But you didn't agree?"

105

"I was never as stupid as them, and never will be either!"

And without taking off his hat, Grey sat on his bench again for a long time. And your soul grew mournful in the dusk from one glance at his hut. In the dusk beyond the wide, snowy gully, Durnovka with its threshing barns and willows in the backyards was drearily black. But as it grew dark, little lights lit up, and it seemed peaceful and cosy inside the huts. And only Grey's hut was unpleasantly black. It was blank, dead. Kuzma already knew: if you went into its dark lobby with the doors ajar, you would feel yourself on the threshold of almost a wild beast's home – it smelt of snow, the gloomy sky was visible through the holes in the roof, the wind rustled at the dung and brushwood tossed up anyhow onto the rafters; if you groped your way to the leaning wall and opened the door, you would encounter cold, darkness, a frozen little window scarcely glimmering in that darkness… There was no one to be seen, but you could guess: the man of the house was on the bench – his pipe showing red like a little coal; the mistress – a submissive, taciturn, slightly mad woman – was quietly rocking a squeaking cradle where a pale child with rickets swung, sleepy from hunger. The kids were huddling on the barely warm stove and telling one another something in an animated whisper. Rustling and fidgeting around in the mouldy straw beneath the plank bed were the nanny goat and the piglet – great friends. You were afraid to straighten up in case you hit your head on the ceiling. You turned with caution too: from the threshold to the opposite wall was just five paces.

"Who's that?" a quiet voice comes out of the darkness.

"Me."

"Kuzma Ilyich, is it?"

"The same."

Grey moves, clears a space on the bench. Kuzma sits down, lights up. Little by little a conversation begins. Depressed by the darkness, Grey is straightforward, sad, confesses to his weaknesses. At times his voice trembles…

The long, snowy winter arrived.

The fields, pale and white under a bluish, gloomy sky, became wider, more expansive and even more desolate. The huts, outbuildings, willows and threshing barns stood out sharply against the first, newly fallen snows. Then blizzards set in and piled up so much snow in drifts that the village took on a wild, northern air, and started having only its doors and windows showing black as they looked out from under white hats pulled well down and from the white depths of the *zavalinkas*. After the blizzards, harsh winds blew across the hardened, grey, icy crust on the fields and tore away the last brown leaves from the shelterless oak thickets in the gullies, and the smallholder Taras Milyayev, who looked like a Siberian and was devoted in the Siberian way to hunting, set off to sink in impassable drifts, dotted all over with the tracks of hares; the water barrels were transformed into frozen blocks; icy, slippery mounds grew up around the ice holes; paths were trampled down through the snowdrifts – and the humdrum life of winter set in. Epidemics began in the village: smallpox, fever, scarlatina... Around the ice holes from which the whole of Durnovka drank, above the stinking, dark bottle-coloured water, peasant women stood for days on end, bent over and with their skirts tucked up above their grey-blue, bare knees, in wet bast shoes, with big, well-wrapped heads. Out of cast-iron pots with ash in them they pulled their own grey petticoats, their men's sackcloth trousers, their children's soiled swaddling clothes, they rinsed them, beat them with rollers and exchanged calls, informing one another that their "hands were red and steaming with the cold", that at the Matyutins' homestead the old granny was dying of a fever, that Yakov's daughter-in-law's throat was blocked up... It was getting dark at three o'clock, and shaggy dogs sat on roofs that were on almost the same level as the snowdrifts. Not a single soul knew what those dogs ate. They were alive, though, and even fierce.

At the manor house they woke up early. At dawn, in the bluish darkness, when little lights were being lit in the huts, stoves were being heated and thick milky smoke was going slowly through the eaves, in the wing with frozen grey windows it got as cold as in the lobby, and Kuzma was woken by the banging of doors and the rustling of the straw, frozen and snowy, which Purse was dragging from a sledge. His quiet, husky voice was heard – the voice of a man who has woken up early and grown cold on an empty stomach. Bride made a clatter with the samovar smokestack and exchanged remarks with Purse in a stern whisper. She slept not in the servants' hut, where the cockroaches drew blood as they ground your arms and legs, but in the hallway, and the whole village was convinced that there was more to this than met the eye. The village knew very well what Bride had been through over the autumn. Taciturn, crushed by the weight of grief, Bride was sterner and sadder than a schema nun. But what of that? Kuzma already knew from Smallholder what they were saying in the village and, waking up, he always remembered it with shame and disgust. He banged on the wall with his fist to let it be known that he was waiting for the samovar and, wheezing, lit up a cigarette: this soothed his heart, eased his chest. He lay beneath his sheepskin coat and, unable to resolve on parting with the warmth, smoked and thought: "Shameless folk! I mean, I've got a daughter of her age..." The fact that a young woman spent the night on the other side of the wall excited in him only fatherly tenderness: in the daytime she was taciturn and serious, sparing of words, and when she was asleep there was something childlike, sad, lonely about her. But could the village believe in that tenderness? Even Tikhon Ilyich didn't: at times he grinned really very strangely indeed. He always had been mistrustful, suspicious, crude in his suspicions, but now he had lost his mind completely: whatever you said to him, he had the same answer to everything.

"Have you heard, Tikhon Ilyich? They say Zakrzhevsky's dying of catarrh: they've taken him to Oryol."

"Lies. We know that catarrh!"

"But it was the medical attendant that was telling me."

"You keep on listening to him..."

Or else you would tell him: "I want to subscribe to a newspaper. Can I have ten roubles or so against my salary, please?"

"Hmm! The man wants to stuff his head full of lies. But to be honest, I've only got fifteen, or maybe twenty kopeks with me..."

Bride would come in with lowered eyelashes:

"We've only got a bit of flour left, Tikhon Ilyich..."

"How's that, then – a bit? Oh, you're lying, woman!"

And he would slant his eyebrows. And while demonstrating how there ought to be enough flour for at least about another three days, he kept on throwing quick glances now at Kuzma, now at Bride. Once he even asked with a grin:

"And how are you sleeping – is it all right, warm?"

And Bride blushed deeply and, bending her head, left the room, while Kuzma's fingers turned cold with shame and anger.

"Shame on you, brother, Tikhon Ilyich," he muttered, turning away to the window. "And especially after what you yourself disclosed to me..."

"So why did she blush?" asked Tikhon Ilyich with a malevolent, embarrassed and awkward smile.

The most unpleasant thing of all in the mornings was getting washed. There was the scent of frost from the straw in the hallway and ice floated like broken glass in the water dispenser. Sometimes Kuzma started on his tea when he had washed only his hands, and he seemed just like an old man after his sleep. The dirt and cold had made him very thin and grey over the autumn. His hands had got lean, the skin on them had become thinner, shinier, and they were covered in little purple spots.

The morning was grey. Under the hardened grey snow the village too was grey. Linen hung like grey, frozen strips of bast on the cross-beams under the roofs of the outbuildings. Beside the huts, where slops were poured out and ashes thrown away, everything froze. Ragged little boys hurried down the street to school between the huts and the outbuildings, running up onto the snowdrifts and sliding down from them in their bast shoes; all of them carried canvas sacks with their slates and bread. Walking towards them, half squatting beneath a yoke with two tubs of water and stepping out awkwardly in ugly felt boots turned hard as wood and covered in pigskin, wearing only an *armyak*, was old, sick, dark-faced Cast-iron; dragging from mound to mound and splashing as it gathered momentum was a water barrel stopped up with straw, behind which ran the white-eyed, stuttering Hambler; women went by on their way to borrow from one another now salt, now millet, now a scoop of flour to make flat cakes or porridge. The threshing floors were empty – only the gates of Yakov's threshing barn were steaming: imitating wealthy peasants, he threshed in winter. And beyond the threshing floors, beyond the bare willows in the backyards, beneath the low, whitish sky unfolded the grey, snowy fields, a wilderness of undulating icy crust.

Sometimes Kuzma went to the servants' hut to join Purse for breakfast – potatoes as hot as fire or sour cabbage soup from the previous day. He recalled the town, where he had spent his whole life, and marvelled: he was not drawn there at all. For Tikhon the town was a sacred dream, he despised and hated the village with all his soul. Kuzma was only making an effort to hate it. Now he looked back on his existence with even greater fear than before: he had grown quite wild in Durnovka

– often he did not wash, did not take his *chuika* off all day, ate from the one bowl with Purse. But worst of all was the fact that, while horrified by his existence, which was ageing him as he watched, he felt that it was nonetheless pleasurable for him, that he seemed to have settled down to precisely the routine which perhaps should really have been his from birth: not for nothing, evidently, did the blood of the men of Durnovka flow in him!

After breakfast he sometimes went for a stroll around the estate or through the village. He visited Yakov's threshing floor, Grey's hut or that of Purse, whose old woman lived alone, was reputed to be a sorceress, was tall and dreadfully thin, big-toothed as death, spoke rudely and resolutely and smoked a pipe like a man: she would heat up the stove, sit down on the plank bed and smoke away, swinging a long, thin foot in a heavy, black bast shoe. Kuzma left the village just a couple of times over the whole period of the fast – he visited the post office and his brother. And both journeys were difficult: Kuzma got so frozen through that he could not feel whether he had a body or not. His sheepskin coat had served so long that it was covered in bald patches. And the wind in the fields was ferocious. After sitting in Durnovka, he could not get enough of the powerful freshness of the winter's air. After long contemplation of the village he was amazed by the snowy-grey expanse, the wintry blue distance seemed to stretch beyond his gaze and to be as beautiful as in a picture. Snorting away, the horse sped cheerfully into the harsh wind, smooth lumps of ice flew with a bang from beneath its iron-shod hooves into the front of the sledge. With a black-and-purple frost-bitten cheek, Purse, grunting cheerfully, leapt down from the box when the sledge swerved, and leapt back onto it sideways at a run. But the wind blew right through you, your feet, resting in straw with snow mixed in, throbbed and grew numb with the cold, your forehead and cheekbones ached... And the low-ceilinged postal office at Ulyanovka was as dreary as only out-of-the-way official government premises can be. It smelt of mould and sealing wax, a ragged postman was banging with a stamp, the sullen Sakharov was yelling at the peasants, angry that Kuzma had not thought to send him half a dozen chickens or a *pood* of flour. Beside Tikhon Ilyich's house he was excited by the smell of steam-engine smoke, it reminded him that the world had towns, people, papers, news. It would have been nice to have a talk with his brother, have a rest at his place and get warm. But the conversation did not go well. His brother was continually being called away, into the store or on household matters, and he only talked about household matters too, and about lies, about the baseness and malice of the peasants and about the need to get rid of the estate as soon as possible. Nastasya Petrovna was pitiful. She had evidently become terribly afraid of her husband; she butted into the conversation inappropriately, praised him inappropriately – his intelligence, his sharp proprietorial eye, the fact that he himself went into absolutely everything thoroughly in household matters.

"He's just so fussy about everything, so fussy!" she said – and Tikhon Ilyich cut her short rudely. After an hour of such conversation Kuzma started to feel drawn back home, to the estate. "He's off his rocker, really and truly, off his rocker!" Kuzma muttered on the way home, remembering Tikhon's sullen, angry face, his reticence, suspicion and the tedious repetition of one and the same thing. And he had a shout at Purse and the horse, in his haste to conceal in his own little home both his melancholy and his old, cold clothing...

At Christmas-tide Ivanushka from Basovo took to visiting Kuzma. He was an old-fashioned peasant turned crazy by longevity, who had once been renowned for his bear-like strength; he was stocky and, now bent double, never lifted his shaggy brown head, and walked with his toes pointing inwards. Ivanushka's entire huge family had died in the cholera outbreak of '92. The sole survivor had been his son, a soldier, who now worked as a trackman on the railway not far from Durnovka. Ivanushka could have lived out the rest of his days with his son, but he preferred to roam around begging. He walked lightly and pigeon-toed across the yard with a staff and hat in his left hand and a sack in the right, with the snow showing white on his uncovered head – and for some reason the sheepdogs did not yap at him. He entered the house and mumbled: "God bless this house and grant it a good master," and sat down on the floor by the wall. Kuzma tore himself away from his book and looked at him over the top of his pince-nez in surprise, in shyness, as if at some beast of the steppe, whose presence in a room was strange. Silently, with lowered eyelashes, with a light, affectionate smile, treading softly in her bast shoes, Bride appeared and gave Ivanushka a bowl of boiled potatoes and a whole hunk of bread, grey with salt, and then stood in the doorway. She wore bast shoes, was firm and broad in the shoulders, and her pretty, wan face had such peasant

111

simplicity and old-timeliness that it seemed she could not possibly have called Ivanushka anything other than grandfather. And smiling – she smiled at him alone – she said quietly:

"Have a bite to eat, have a bite to eat, Grandfather."

And he, without raising his head, knowing of her affection only through her voice, moaned softly in reply, and sometimes mumbled: "The Lord keep you, Granddaughter," crossing himself with a gesture broad and awkward, as if with a paw, and greedily set about the food. On his brown hair, inhumanly dense and thick, the snow was melting. Water ran across the floor from his bast shoes. From his threadbare brown *chekmen*, worn over a dirty hempen shirt, came the smoky smell of a hut with no chimney. His hands, disfigured by long years of work, with gnarled, inflexible fingers, caught hold of the potatoes with difficulty.

"I expect it's cold just wearing a *chekmen*?" asked Kuzma loudly.

"Eh?" Ivanushka responded in a weak moan, raising an ear that was covered in hair.

"I expect you're cold?"

Ivanushka had a think.

"Why cold?" he replied deliberately. "Not cold at all... In the old days it was bitterer by far."

"Lift your head up, smooth your hair out!"

Ivanushka slowly shook his head.

"Can't lift it now, brother... Bent to the ground..."

And with a dim smile, he made an effort to lift his ugly, hairy face and his tiny little screwed-up eyes.

Having eaten his fill, he sighed, crossed himself, gathered up the crumbs from his lap and finished chewing them; then he groped about next to him, searching for the sack, staff and hat, but when he had found them, reassured, he began an unhurried conversation. He could sit in silence the whole day, but Kuzma and Bride asked him questions, and, as if dreaming, from somewhere a long way off, he answered them. He told in his clumsy, antiquated language of how the Tsar was made entirely of gold, that the Tsar couldn't eat fish – "terribly salty" – that the prophet Elijah once broke through the sky and fell to earth – "he was terribly bulky"; that John the Baptist was born as shaggy as a sheep and would hit the person he was baptising on the head with an iron crutch to make him "come to his senses"; that once a year, on

Flor and Lavr's Day,* every horse tried to kill someone; he told how the rye in the olden days was so dense that a grass snake couldn't crawl through it, that they used to mow two *desyatins* a day per brother; that he used to have a gelding which they kept "on a shain", it was so strong and fearsome; that once, about sixty years ago, he, Ivanushka, had had such a fine horse collar stolen, he would not have taken two roubles for it... He was firmly convinced that his family had died not of cholera, but because they had moved into a new hut after a fire and had spent the night in it without having first let the chanticleer do so, and that he and his son had been saved only by chance: he had been sleeping in the threshing barn... Towards evening Ivanushka got up and left, paying no attention to any kind of weather and without yielding to any exhortations to stay until morning... And he caught his death of cold and died, just before Epiphany, in his son's hut. His son tried to persuade him to receive the Eucharist. Ivanushka would not agree: he said that once you'd received it, you'd die, and he had taken a firm decision "not to give in" to death. He lay senseless for days on end, but even when delirious he begged his daughter-in-law to say he was not at home if death came knocking. Once, in the night, he came round, gathered his strength, climbed off the stove and knelt down before an icon, lit up by an icon lamp. He sighed heavily and mumbled for a long time, repeating: "Lord and Father, forgive my trespusses"... Then he fell into thought and was silent for a long time with his head pressed against the floor. And suddenly he got up and said firmly: "No, I won't give in!" But in the morning he saw that his daughter-in-law was rolling out pies and stoking the stove up hot...

"Is that for my funeral?" he asked in a faltering voice.

The daughter-in-law remained silent. Again he gathered his strength, again he climbed off the stove, went out into the lobby: yes, right enough – standing upright against the wall was a huge purple coffin with white, eight-pointed crosses! Then he remembered what had happened some thirty years before to his neighbour, old Lukyan: Lukyan had fallen ill, a coffin had been bought for him – a good, expensive coffin too – flour, vodka, salted pikeperch had been brought from town, and Lukyan had gone and recovered. What was to be done with the coffin? How was the expenditure to be justified? For some five years afterwards Lukyan had been cursed for it, had been driven to death with reproaches... Remembering this, Ivanushka hung his head and trudged resignedly into

113

the hut. And in the night, lying senseless on his back, he began singing in a tremulous, plaintive voice, but ever quieter and quieter – and suddenly his knees started shaking, he started to hiccup, a deep breath lifted his chest high, and, with froth on his opened lips, he fell still...

Kuzma spent almost a month in bed because of Ivanushka. On the morning of Epiphany they said it was so cold that a bird might freeze on the wing, and Kuzma did not even have felt boots. But he went to take a last look at the dead man all the same. His hands, stiff and folded below his huge chest on a clean hempen shirt, disfigured by horny growths from eighty whole years of primevally hard work, were so coarse and ugly that Kuzma made haste to turn away. And he could not even throw a sidelong glance at Ivanushka's hair, at his bestial, dead face – he hurriedly threw the white calico back over it. To get warm, he drank some vodka and sat for a while in front of the hotly glowing stove. The hut was cosy and festively clean, and above the head of the wide, purple coffin, covered with calico, there glimmered the golden light of a wax candle, stuck onto the dark icon in the corner, and there shone the bright colours of a popular print – Joseph being sold by his brothers. The ex-soldier's affable wife picked up cast-iron pots weighing a *pood* on an oven fork and moved them into the stove with ease, talked cheerily about the firewood that came with the job, and kept on asking him to stay until her husband's return from the village. But Kuzma was feverish; his face was burning, and the vodka, which had spread through his frozen body like poison, made unmotivated tears begin welling up in his eyes... And without getting warm, Kuzma set off over the firm, white waves of the fields for Tikhon Ilyich's. The rime-covered, bushy-white gelding ran fast, snarling and choking with spleen, throwing shafts of grey steam out of its nostrils; the sledge wailed, its iron runner bindings squealing resonantly over the harsh snow; behind, in frosty rings, the low sun was yellow; from ahead, from the north, came a burning wind that took the breath away; mileposts bowed in the thick, bushy rime, and large grey buntings flew in a flock in front of the gelding, scattered down over the glossy road, pecked at the frozen dung, flew up again, and again scattered down. Kuzma gazed at them through heavy white eyelashes, felt that his face had become stiff with cold and, with the white curls of his moustache and beard, had begun to resemble a mummer's mask... The sun was setting, and the waves of snow were a deathly green in the orange glow, and extending from their crests and jagged edges were pale-blue shadows... Kuzma turned the horse sharply and drove it back, towards home. The sun set, in the house with its grey, snow-covered window panes a dim light was glimmering, there was blue-grey gloom, it was desolate and cold. The bullfinch which had hung in a cage beside the window looking out onto the garden had died, and it lay with its legs in the air, its feathers fluffed up, its little red craw blown out.

"Finished!" said Kuzma, and took the bullfinch to throw it away.

Durnovka, covered in frozen snow, so far from the whole world on this sad evening in the midst of the steppe winter, suddenly horrified him. This is the end! His burning head was dull and heavy, he would lie down now and not get up again... With her bast shoes squeaking over the snow, Bride was coming towards the porch with a bucket in her hand.

"I'm ill, Dunyushka!" said Kuzma affectionately, in the hope of hearing an affectionate word from her.

But Bride answered indifferently, drily:

"Get the samovar going, should I?"

And didn't even ask what was wrong with him. Didn't ask anything about Ivanushka either... Kuzma returned to the dark room and, trembling all over, wondering in horror how and where he was going to go to relieve himself now, he lay down on the couch... And the evenings got mixed up with the nights, the nights with the days, and all count of them was lost.

On the first night, at about three o'clock, he came round and banged his fist on the wall to ask for some water: in his sleep he had been tormented by thirst and by wondering whether the bullfinch had been thrown away. But no one responded to the banging. Bride had gone off to spend the night in the servants' hut. And Kuzma remembered that he was on the verge of dying, he felt it, and he was seized by such anguish, as though he had come round in a burial vault. So the hallway, smelling of snow, straw and horse collars, was empty! So he, sick and helpless, was entirely alone in this dark, icy little house, where the windows were dimly grey amidst the deathly quiet of the endless winter's night, and a cage was hanging there needlessly!

"Lord, save me and have mercy, Lord, help me just a little," he whispered, lifting himself up and rummaging through his pockets with trembling hands.

He wanted to light a match. But his whispering was feverish, there was noise and ringing in his blazing head, his hands and feet were like ice... Klasha came, quickly threw the door open, lay his head on the pillow and sat down on a chair beside the couch... She was dressed like a young lady – a velvet fur coat, a hat and muff of white fur – her hands smelt of perfume, her eyes shone, her cheeks were all red from the frost... "Ah, how well everything's been resolved!" someone whispered, but it was not so good that for some reason Klasha did not light the light, that she had come not to see him, but for Ivanushka's funeral... that she suddenly began singing in a bass voice to a guitar accompaniment: "Daring Khaz-Bulat, your mountain hut is poor..."

In the deadly anguish that poisoned his soul at the start of the illness, Kuzma raved about the bullfinch, Klasha, Voronezh, but even in his ravings he was never abandoned by the idea of telling someone they should at least take pity on him in one respect and not bury him at Kolodezi. But my God, wasn't it madness to hope for pity in Durnovka? Once he came to his senses in the morning, while they were heating the stove, and the simple, calm voices of Purse and Bride seemed to him as merciless, alien and strange as the day-to-day life of the healthy always seems merciless, alien and strange to the sick. He wanted to cry out, to ask them to get the samovar going – but he was struck dumb: he heard the angry whisper of Purse, who was talking, of course, about him, the sick man, and Bride's curt reply:

"Oh, bother him! When he dies, he'll be buried..."

Afterwards, the late afternoon sun shone into the windows through the bare branches of the acacias. There was blue tobacco smoke. Beside the bed sat the old medical attendant, smelling of medicines and frosty freshness, pulling icicles from his moustache. The samovar was boiling on the table, and Tikhon Ilyich, tall, grey-haired, stern, was standing at the table brewing fragrant tea. The medical attendant was talking of his cows, the price of flour and butter, and Tikhon Ilyich was recounting how wonderful, how rich Nastasya Petrovna's funeral had been, and how glad he was that a buyer had at last been found for Durnovka. Kuzma understood that Tikhon Ilyich was fresh from town, that Nastasya Petrovna had died there suddenly, on the way to the station; he understood that the funeral had cost Tikhon Ilyich terribly dear and that he had already taken a deposit on Durnovka – and he was utterly indifferent...

Waking up one day very late and feeling only weakness, he sat down at the samovar. The day was overcast, warm, a lot of fresh snow was piling up. Leaving in it the prints of his bast shoes, dotted with little crosses, Grey went past by the window. The sheepdogs ran around him, sniffing at his ragged coat-tails. And he was pulling along by the reins a tall, dirty light-bay horse, ugly from old age and thinness, with shoulders rubbed raw by collars, a battered back and a sparse, unclean tail. It was hobbling on three legs and dragging the fourth, which was broken below the knee. And Kuzma remembered that Tikhon Ilyich had been there three days before and said he had ordered Grey to give the sheepdogs a treat, to find an old horse and to slaughter it, he remembered that Grey had earned his living at times before by this business – the purchase of dead or worthless livestock for their hides. Not long ago, something terrible had happened to Grey, Tikhon Ilyich had said: when preparing to slaughter a mare, Grey had forgotten to hobble it, and only its head had been tied up and pulled to one side, and as soon as he had crossed himself and struck a slender little knife into the vein beside the collarbone, the mare had let out a shriek and, shrieking, with its yellow teeth bared in pain and rage, and a stream of black blood gushing onto the snow, it had hurled itself at its killer and chased after him for a long time like a man – and it would have caught him, but "thankfully the snow was deep"… Kuzma had been so struck by this incident that now, glancing out of the window, he again felt a heaviness in his legs. He started swallowing hot tea, and gradually recovered. He had a smoke, had a sit down… Finally he got up, went out into the hallway and glanced at the bare, sparse garden beyond the thawed-out window: in the garden, on the snow-white blanket of the glade, was the red of a big-sided, bloody carcass with a long neck and a skinned head; the dogs, hunched over and straining their paws against the meat, were greedily ripping out the guts and pulling them about; two old blue-black ravens were hopping sideways towards the head, taking off when the growling dogs flung themselves at them, then coming down again onto the virgin-white snow. "Ivanushka, Grey, the ravens…" thought Kuzma. "Lord, save me and have mercy, take me away from here!"

The indisposition stayed with Kuzma for a long time yet. He was sadly and joyously touched by the thought of spring, he wanted to get out of Durnovka fast. He knew that the end of winter could not be expected yet, but thaws were already starting. The first week of February was dark and misty. The mist hid the fields, ate up the snow. The village was black, water stood between dirty snowdrifts; the district policeman rode straight through the village one day completely bespattered with horse droppings. The cocks were crowing, and from the ventilator came the smell of the exciting dampness of spring... He still wanted to live – to live, to wait for the spring and a move to town, to live, submitting to fate, and to do any kind of work at all, if only for a crust of bread... And of course, with his brother – whatever he might be like. After all, his brother had already suggested to him while he had been sick that he should move to Vorgol.

"How can I possibly turn you out," he had said, after having a think. "From the first of March I'm passing on the store and the yard too – let's go to town, brother dear, well away from these cut-throats!"

And it was true: they were cut-throats. Smallholder came and passed on the details of a recent thing that had happened to Grey. Deniska had returned from Tula and was loafing about doing nothing, saying in the village that he wanted to get married, that he had some money and would soon be starting a new life, a top-class one. At first the village called these likely tales lies, then, from Deniska's hints, it grasped what was going on and began believing. Grey began believing too, and started to try and ingratiate himself with his son. But having skinned the horse and had a rouble from Tikhon Ilyich and got a fifty-kopek piece for the hide, he cocked his nose and went on a spree: he drank for two days, lost his pipe and lay down to rest up on the stove. His head ached, and he had nothing to smoke from. And so in order to roll cigarettes, he started peeling off the newspapers and various pictures with which Deniska had papered the ceiling. He did this in secret, of course, but one day Deniska caught him at it anyway. Caught him and started yelling. Grey, with a hangover, started yelling too – and Deniska dragged him off the stove and was beating the life out of him until the neighbours came running... But, thought Kuzma, isn't Tikhon Ilyich a cut-throat too, insisting with the obstinacy of a madman on Bride's wedding to one of these cut-throats!

On hearing about this wedding for the first time, Kuzma had firmly resolved not to allow it. What an awful, what an absurd thing! Then, coming to his senses during his illness, he had even rejoiced at that absurd thing. He was surprised and shocked by Bride's indifference to him, a sick man. "A beast, a savage!" he thought and, remembering the wedding, he added maliciously: "A good thing too! Serves her right!"

Now, after the illness, both the resolve and the malice had disappeared. One day he began talking to Bride about Tikhon Ilyich's intention, and she calmly replied:

"Why, I've already been chatting with Tikhon Ilyich about that business. May God grant him good health, it was a good idea of his."

"Good?" said Kuzma in amazement.

Bride looked at him and shook her head:

"Well, what isn't good about it? You're a strange one, honest to God, Kuzma Ilyich! He's promising money, taking the wedding upon himself... And again, he's not thought of some widower or other, but a young fellow, without any vices... not half-dead, not a drunkard..."

"But an idler, a bruiser, an arrant fool," added Kuzma.

Bride cast her eyes down and was silent for a moment. She sighed and, turning around, went towards the door.

"Whatever you like," she said, with a tremor in her voice. "That's your business... Try and break it off... So be it."

Kuzma opened his eyes wide and shouted:

"Hang on, you're out of your mind! Do you think I wish you ill?"

Bride turned and stopped.

"Don't you, then?" she began hotly and rudely, blushing red and with her eyes flashing. "Where am I to go, in your view? Pestering people on their doorsteps for ever? Feeding off someone else's crusts? Roaming around as a homeless beggar? Or looking for a widower, an old man? Haven't I swallowed enough tears?"

And her voice broke. She started crying and left the room. In the evening Kuzma convinced her that he was not even thinking of breaking the arrangement, and finally she believed him, and gave a shy and affectionate smile.

"Well, thank you," she said in the nice tone in which she used to speak to Ivanushka.

But here too tears began to tremble on her eyelashes – and Kuzma again spread his hands.

"And what is it now?"

And Bride quietly replied:

"There'll probably be no great joy with Deniska either..."

Purse brought almost a month and a half's newspapers from the post office. The days were dark and misty, and Kuzma read from morning till evening, sitting by the window. And when he had finished he was rooted

119

to the spot, stunned by the number of new executions. White, granular snow was slanting down fast, falling onto the black, impoverished little village, onto the bumpy, muddy roads, onto the horse dung, ice and water; a dusky mist hid the fields...

"Avdotya!" Kuzma shouted, getting up from his place. "Tell Purse to harness the horse to the sledge!"

Tikhon Ilyich was at home. He was sitting at the samovar in just a calico *kosovorotka*, swarthy, with a white beard, with knitted grey eyebrows, big and strong, and he was brewing tea.

"Ah! Brother dear!" he exclaimed affably, without moving his brows apart. "You've returned to God's earth? Careful now, isn't it a bit early?"

"I've really missed you, brother," Kuzma replied, kissing him.

"Well, if you've missed me, then let's warm ourselves and have a chat..."

After asking one another if there was any news, they started drinking their tea in silence and then each lit up a cigarette.

"You've grown very thin, brother dear!" said Tikhon Ilyich, stretching and looking at Kuzma from under his brows.

"One would do," replied Kuzma quietly. "Don't you read the newspapers?"

Tikhon Ilyich grinned.

"Those lies? No, God forbid."

"So many executions, if only you knew!"

"Executions? Quite right too... Have you heard what happened near Yelets? At the Bykov brothers' farm?... You must remember them, the ones with a burr. These Bykovs are sitting there, no different to us, round about evening time, playing draughts... Suddenly – what's that? Someone tramping on the porch, shouting: 'Open up!' And those Bykovs, they didn't have the time, brother of mine, to bat an eyelid, before in bursts their workman, a wretch of a peasant the likes of Grey, and after him two ruffians of some sort, to put it briefly, greenhorns... And all with crowbars. They raised the crowbars, and then they started yelling: 'Get yer 'ands up, motherfuckers!' The Bykovs had the fright of their lives, of course, leapt up shouting: 'What's all this about?' But the wretch of a peasant kept on: get 'em up, get 'em up!"

And Tikhon Ilyich gave a gloomy smile and, becoming thoughtful, fell silent.

"Well, go on and finish," said Kuzma.

"There's nothing to finish… They put their hands up, of course, and ask: 'What do you want?' – 'Give us some ham! Where are your keys?' – 'You son of a bitch! As if you don't know! There they are, on the lintel, hanging on the nail…'"

"This is with their hands up?" Kuzma interrupted.

"Of course it is… Well, and they'll give them hell for those hands now! They'll hang them, of course. They're already in jail, the little darlings…"

"That's for the ham they'll hang them?"

"No, for buggery, forgive me, Lord, my trespass," responded Tikhon Ilyich, half-angrily, half-jokingly. "For God's sake stop being prickly and passing yourself off as Balashkin! It's time you gave it up…"

Kuzma fingered his little grey beard. His worn-out, thin face, his mournful eyes, his crookedly raised left eyebrow were reflected in the mirror, and, after taking a look at himself, he quietly agreed:

"Being prickly? You're right, it's time… it's high time…"

And Tikhon Ilyich turned the conversation to business. He had evidently become thoughtful a little while before, in the middle of his account, only because he had remembered something much more important than executions – some sort of business.

"Now I've already told Deniska he should finish this here tune as soon as possible," he began firmly, distinctly and sternly, sprinkling tea into the teapot from his cupped hand. "And I'm asking you, brother dear, to take a part in it, this here tune. It's awkward for me, you see. And after that, you move in here. It'll be grand, brother dear! As we've already decided to wind everything up completely, there's no reason for you to sit there to no purpose. It's only double the expense. And once you've moved, get yourself in harness next to me. We'll throw the weight off our shoulders, get ourselves, God grant, to town, and start up a grain-collecting station. There's no room to expand in this godforsaken hole. We'll shake its dust off our feet, and then let it go to hell. I'm not going to die here! Bear it in mind," he said, knitting his brows, stretching out his arms and clenching his fists, "you won't slip away from me yet, not from me, it's still too soon for me to be lying on the stove! I'll put the Devil in his place!"

Kuzma listened, gazing almost in fear at his fixed, mad eyes, at his twisted mouth, rapping out the words in predatory fashion – he listened and was silent. Then he asked:

"Brother, for Christ's sake tell me, what are you getting out of this wedding? I don't understand it, as God's my witness, I don't. I simply can't bear the sight of your Deniska. This nice new type, the new Rus, it'll outdo all the old ones. Ignore the fact that he's bashful, sentimental and pretends to be a fool – he's such a cynical animal! He talks about me and says I'm sleeping with Bride…"

"Really, you just never know when to stop," Tikhon Ilyich interrupted with a frown. "You harp on about it yourself: the unfortunate people, the unfortunate people! And now – he's an animal!"

"Yes, I do and will harp on!" Kuzma chimed in hotly. "But I'm at my wits' end! I don't understand anything now: either they're unfortunate, or else… Now listen: I mean, Deniska, you hate him yourself! You both hate each other! He never calls you anything other than a 'cut-throat who's eaten into the people's withers', and you curse *him* as a cut-throat! He boasts brazenly in the village that he's the King's best friend now…"

"I know he does!" Tikhon Ilyich interrupted again.

"And do you know what he says about Bride?" Kuzma continued, not listening. "You see, she has such a delicate, white complexion, and he, the animal, do you know what he says? 'White as marble, the bitch!' And will you finally understand one thing: he won't stay in the village, you know, you won't keep him in the village now, the tramp, with a lasso. Him, the master of the house, him, a family man? As he walked through the village yesterday I heard him singing in his fucking little voice: 'So fine like an andel from heaven, like a deman so artful and bad…'"*

"I know!" shouted Tikhon Ilyich. "He won't stay in the village, not for anything he won't! Well, and to hell with him! And as for his not being the master of the house, well you and I are such good ones! I remember I'm talking to you about business – in the tavern, you remember? – and you're listening to the quail… But next, what's next?"

"What do you mean, what? And what's the quail got to do with it?" asked Kuzma.

Tikhon Ilyich drummed his fingers on the table for a while and rapped out sternly, clearly:

"Bear it in mind: mill the wind and it'll still be wind. My word is sacred for ever and aye. Once I've said it, I'll do it. I won't light a candle for my sin, but do a good deed. I may only offer one mite, but for that mite the Lord will remember me."

Kuzma leapt up from his place.

"The Lord, the Lord!" he exclaimed in a falsetto. "What sort of Lord do we have? What sort of Lord can be had by Deniska, Akimka, Menshov, Grey, you and me?"

"Hang on," Tikhon Ilyich asked sternly. "Who's this Akimka?"

"There I lay dying," Kuzma continued, not listening, "did I think about Him much? I thought just the one thing: I don't know anything about Him, and I don't know how to think!" shouted Kuzma. "I've not been taught!"

And looking around with darting eyes that were full of suffering, doing up and undoing his buttons, he walked across the room and stopped right in front of Tikhon Ilyich's face.

"Remember this, brother," he said, and his cheekbones flushed. "Remember this: our song is over. And no candles are going to save you and me. Do you hear? We're men of Durnovka!"

And rendered speechless by his agitation, he fell silent. But Tikhon Ilyich was already thinking his own thoughts again, and suddenly he agreed:

"It's true. They're no good for any damned thing! Just think..."

And he grew animated, carried away by a new thought:

"Just think: they've been ploughing for all of a thousand years – no, what am I saying! More! But there's not a single soul knows how to do it properly! They don't know when they need to go out into the fields! When to sow, when to mow! 'We do the same as everyone else' – it's as simple as that. Mark my words!" he shouted sternly, knitting his brows, as Kuzma had shouted at him before. "'We do the same as everyone else!' Not a single woman knows how to bake bread – the whole top crust falls off, damn it, and under the crust it's sour water!"

And Kuzma was taken aback. His thoughts became confused.

"He's off his rocker!" he thought, following his brother with senseless eyes as he lit the lamp.

But Tikhon Ilyich did not allow him to collect himself and continued excitedly:

"The people! They're foul-mouthed, idle liars, and so shameless that they don't trust each other, not one of them! Mark my words," he yelled, not seeing that the wick he had lit was blazing and belching soot almost to the very ceiling, "not us, but each other! And they're all like

123

that, all of them!" he cried in a plaintive voice, and put the glass onto the lamp with a crack.

It had turned blue outside the windows. Young, white snow was flying onto the puddles and the snowdrifts. Kuzma watched it and was silent. The conversation had taken such an unexpected turn that even Kuzma's fervour had gone. Not knowing what to say, not daring to glance into his brother's mad eyes, he started rolling a cigarette.

"Off his rocker," he thought hopelessly. "But it serves him right. What does it matter!"

Tikhon Ilyich lit a cigarette and started to calm down too. He took a seat and, gazing at the light of the lamp, he muttered quietly:

"And you say 'Deniska'... Have you heard what Makar Ivanovich, the wanderer, did? He and his mate caught a woman on the road, dragged her off to a watchman's hut in Klyuchiki, and spent four days going there and raping her... by turns. Well, now they're in jail..."

"Tikhon Ilyich," said Kuzma affectionately, "what's this rubbish you're talking? What's the point? You must be unwell. You're jumping from one thing to another, saying one thing one moment, and a minute later another... Drinking a lot, are you?"

Tikhon Ilyich remained silent. He just waved a hand, and in the eyes staring at the light, tears began to tremble.

"Are you drinking?" Kuzma repeated quietly.

"Yes," Tikhon Ilyich answered quietly. "Who wouldn't be? Do you think it was easy getting this golden cage? Do you think it's been easy living my whole life as a watchdog, and with an old woman too? I've had no pity for anyone, brother dear... Well, and I've not been shown much pity either! Do you think I don't know how they hate me? Do you think they wouldn't have killed me viciously if they'd really got it into their heads, those peasants, if they'd got lucky in that revolution? Just wait, just wait – it'll happen, it will! We've done for them!"

"And the hanging for the ham?" asked Kuzma.

"Well, the hanging," responded Tikhon Ilyich in a voice full of suffering. "I didn't really mean it, it just came out as I was talking..."

"But hang them they will!"

"Well, that's no business of ours. They'll have to answer to the Almighty."

And knitting his brows, he fell into thought and closed his eyes.

"Ah," he said with a deep sigh and in a grief-stricken voice. "Ah, dear brother of mine! Soon, soon, we too will face judgement before His throne. I read the Book of Needs in the evenings, and I weep, I wail over that there book. I just marvel at it: how could such sweet words have been thought up! Here, wait…"

And he quickly rose, took a thick book in a church binding out from behind the mirror, put on his glasses with trembling hands and, with tears in his voice, hurriedly, as if afraid of being interrupted, he began reading:

"I weep and I wail when I think upon death, and behold our beauty, fashioned after the image of God, lying in the tomb, disfigured, dishonoured, bereft of form…

"Of a truth, all things are vanity, and life is but a shadow and a dream. For in vain doth everyone who is born of earth disquiet himself, as saith the Scriptures: when we have acquired the world, then do we take up our abode in the grave, where kings and beggars lie down together…"*

"Kings and beggars!" Tikhon Ilyich repeated in rapturous sorrow, and shook his head. "My life's lost, brother dear! I had a mute cook once, you see, and I gave the idiot a foreign-made shawl, *and she went and wore holes in it turned inside out*… You see? Out of stupidity and meanness. It's a waste to have the right side showing on ordinary days, like, I'll wait for a holiday – but when the holiday came, there were only rags left… And I've done the same… *with my life*. It's truly so!"

While returning to Durnovka, Kuzma felt one thing alone – dull anguish. And in dull anguish passed all of his last days in Durnovka.

It snowed during those days, and snow was all they had been waiting for in Grey's homestead, for the road to the wedding to improve.

On the 12th of February, towards evening, in the gloom of the cold hallway, a quiet conversation took place. By the stove stood Bride, with a yellow and black dotted headscarf pulled down over her forehead, gazing at her bast shoes. By the doors was short-legged Deniska, hatless, in the heavy *poddyovka* with drooping shoulders. He was looking down as well, at the ankle boots with metal heel taps he was twisting in his hands. The boots belonged to Bride. Deniska had mended them and come to get five kopeks for the work.

"I haven't got it," said Bride. "And Kuzma Ilyich seems to have fallen asleep. Wait until tomorrow."

"I can't wait, see," Deniska replied in a pensive, sing-song voice, picking at the heel tap with his fingernail.

"Well, what are we to do now?"

Deniska had a think, sighed and, giving his thick hair a shake, he suddenly raised his head.

"Well, why prattle on for nothing," he said loudly and decisively, not looking at Bride and overcoming his bashfulness. "Has Tikhon Ilyich spoken to you?"

"He has," replied Bride. "I'm even sick of him."

"Then I'll come back straight away with my father. Kuzma Ilyich will soon be getting up to have tea anyway…"

Bride had a think.

"That's your business…"

Deniska put the boots down on the window sill and left without any further reminder about the money. And half an hour later the stamping of bast shoes having the snow knocked off them could be heard from the porch: Deniska had returned with Grey – and for some reason Grey had a red sash around his *chekmen*, around his hips. Kuzma came out to see them. Deniska and Grey spent a long time crossing themselves in the direction of a dark corner, then gave their hair a shake and lifted their faces.

"Whether you're the father of the bride-to-be or not, you're still a good man!" Grey began unhurriedly in an unusually relaxed and agreeable tone. "You have to give away an adopted daughter, I have to find a wife for my son. Let us in good accord have speech between us for the sake of their happiness."

And he gave a sober, low bow.

Restraining a pained smile, Kuzma asked for Bride to be called.

"Run and find her," Grey ordered Deniska in a whisper, as if in church.

"I'm here," Bride said, coming out from behind the door, from the direction of the stove, and bowed to Grey.

Silence fell. The samovar, which stood on the floor with its grille showing red in the darkness, was boiling and bubbling. No faces were visible.

"Well then, daughter, you decide," said Kuzma, grinning.

Bride had a think.

"I've nothing against the lad…"

126

"And you, Denis?"

Deniska paused too.

"Well, I've got to marry some time anyway... P'raps, God grant, this'll do..."

And the fathers congratulated one another on getting the business started. The samovar was taken away to the servants' hut. Smallholder, who had heard the news before anyone else and come running from the Ridge, lit the lamp in the servants' hut, sent Purse to get vodka and sunflower heads, sat the bride and groom down under an icon, poured tea for them, sat down herself next to Grey and, to dispel the awkwardness, began singing in a high, shrill voice, throwing glances at Deniska, at his sallow face and big eyelashes:

> Now through our garden,
> Through the green grapes,
> A young man he did stroll,
> Comely, white as white...

The next day, everyone who heard about this feast from Grey smirked and advised: "You might have given the young couple a bit of help!" Purse said the same as well: "Their life's just beginning, you have to help the young couple." Grey went off home in silence and brought Bride, who was ironing in the hallway, two cast-iron pots and a ball of black thread.

"Here, daughter-in-law," he said in embarrassment, "take these, your mother-in-law sent them. Maybe they'll be of some use... We've got nothing, you know – if we did have, I'd bend over backwards..."

Bride bowed and thanked him. She was ironing the curtain sent by Tikhon Ilyich "in place of a veil", and her eyes were damp and red. Grey wanted to comfort her and said it wasn't "all milk and honey" for him either, but hesitated, sighed and, putting the pots down on the window sill, he left the house.

"I've put the thread in one of the pots," he mumbled.

"Thank you, Father," Bride thanked him again in that affectionate and special tone she had used only with Ivanushka, and, as soon as Grey had gone, she unexpectedly smiled a faint, mocking smile and began to sing: "Now through our garden..."

Kuzma poked his head out of the reception hall and looked at her sternly over the top of his pince-nez. She fell quiet.

"Listen," said Kuzma. "Maybe this whole business should be dropped?"

"It's too late now," Bride answered quietly. "The shame can't be avoided anyway... Doesn't everyone know whose money we're going to be feasting on? And the spending's already begun..."

Kuzma shrugged his shoulders. True, along with the curtain Tikhon Ilyich had sent twenty-five roubles, a sack of coarse flour, some millet and a thin pig... But you didn't have to ruin your life because this pig had already been slaughtered!

"Oh dear," said Kuzma. "You've worn me out! 'The shame, the spending'... And do you think you're worth less than the pig?"

"Worth less or not, you can't bring the dead back from the graveyard," Bride answered simply and firmly, and, sighing, she neatly folded the warm, ironed curtain. "Will you have dinner now?"

Her face had become calm. "Well, no more of it, you won't get anywhere with this!" Kuzma thought, and said:

"Well, you must try and make the best of it..."

After having dinner, he smoked and looked out of the window. It was getting dark. In the servants' hut, he knew, they had already baked a rye plait, "a ritual pie". They were preparing to cook two pots of brawn, a pot of noodles, a pot of cabbage soup and a pot of porridge – all made from the slaughtered pig. And Grey was busy on the snowy mound between the barns and the shed. On the mound, in the bluish twilight, the straw piled on top of the slaughtered pig was blazing with an orange flame. Around the flame, waiting for spoils, sat the sheepdogs, and their white faces and chests were silky and pink. Grey, sinking in the snow, was running about, adjusting the bonfire, waving his arms threateningly at the sheepdogs. He had opened out and lifted up the skirts of his homespun coat and tucked them into his belt, he kept pushing his hat onto the back of his head with the wrist of his right hand, in which there gleamed a knife. Briefly and brightly lit up now from one side, now from the other, Grey threw a large, dancing shadow onto the snow – the shadow of a pagan. Then past the barn and down the track towards the village, disappearing behind the snowy mound, ran Smallholder, going to summon the women who sang at weddings and to ask Dowdy for the fir tree she kept in the cellar and which went from one hen party to the next. And when Kuzma had dressed himself, combing his hair and changing his jacket with holes in the elbows for his cherished long-tailed frock coat, and emerged onto the porch, white now from the falling snow, in the soft, grey darkness, by the lighted windows of the servants' hut there was already a big black crowd of girls, lads and little boys, there was a din, the sound of voices and of people playing three accordions at once, and all different tunes. Kuzma, hunched up, pulling at his fingers and cracking them, got as far as the crowd, pushed his way through and, bending down, went into the dark, into the lobby. The lobby was crowded and cramped too. Little boys were darting about between people's legs, they were being grabbed by the neck and shoved out – and then they would try to get back in again…

"Let me in, for God's sake!" said Kuzma, squashed at the doors.

He was squashed even more – and somebody tugged the door open. In clouds of steam he stepped over the threshold and stopped in the doorway. The people clustered here were rather cleaner – girls in flowery shawls, lads in all new clothing. It smelt of fine cloth, sheepskin coats, paraffin, cheap tobacco, pine needles. A little green tree decorated with scraps of red calico stood on the table, extending its branches above a dim tin lamp. Around the table, beneath the small, wet, thawed-out windows, by the black, damp walls, sat the singers in their finery, crudely rouged and powdered, with shining eyes, all in silk and woollen headscarves, with iridescent, curling feathers from a drake's tail stuck into their hair at the temples. At the very moment when Kuzma entered, Dowdy, a lame girl with a dark, bad-tempered, intelligent face, with black, sharp eyes and black eyebrows that met in the middle, struck up an old ritual song in a coarse, strong voice:

In our village in the evening, in the evening,
At the evening's final end,
At Avdotya's hen party…

In an amicable, dissonant chorus, the girls caught up her last words – and everyone turned to the bride-to-be: she was sitting, according to custom, beside the stove, unadorned, with her head covered in a dark shawl, and she was to reply to the song with loud crying and ritual lamentations: "My dear Father, Mother dear, how am I to live my life, grieve my grief in marriage?" But the bride-to-be was silent. And the girls, finishing the song, gave her a discontented sidelong glance.

129

Then they whispered among themselves and, frowning, slowly and lingeringly began to sing "the orphan's song":

> Get heated, little bathhouse,
> Strike, you ringing bell!

And Kuzma's firmly clenched jaws began to tremble, a cold shiver ran over his head and shins, his cheekbones started aching sweetly, and his eyes filled and grew dim with tears. The bride-to-be wrapped herself up in her shawl and suddenly started shaking all over with sobs.

"That's enough, girls," someone shouted.

But the girls paid no attention:

> Strike, you ringing bell,
> Wake my father up...

And with a groan, the bride-to-be started to let her face drop onto her knees, into her hands, choking on her tears... She was finally led away, trembling and staggering, into the unheated part of the hut, to be dressed up.

And then Kuzma blessed her. The groom arrived with Vaska, Yakov's son. The groom had put the latter's boots on; the groom's hair had been trimmed, and his neck, bordered by the lace collar of his blue shirt, was red from shaving. He had washed with soap and looked very much younger, and was even not bad-looking, and, knowing this, he was lowering his dark eyelashes modestly and soberly. When Vaska, the best man, came in, wearing a red shirt and an unfastened Romanov-style sheepskin coat, he threw a stern sidelong glance at the singers.

"Enough of that bawling!" he said rudely, and added what was required according to ritual: "Come on out, come on out."

The singers replied in a chorus:

"It takes three to build a house, four corners to roof a hut. Put a rouble in each corner and a fifth in the middle with vodka."

Vaska drew a half-*shtof** bottle from his pocket and set it on the table. The girls picked it up and rose. It became even more cramped. Again the door flew open, again there was a rush of steam and cold, and, pushing people aside, in came Smallholder with a little foil icon, and after her the bride, in a pale-blue dress with frills, and everyone gasped: she was so pale, calm and beautiful. Swinging his arm, Vaska gave a whack on the forehead to a little lad with broad shoulders, a big head and crooked legs like a dachshund's, and he flung someone's old sheepskin jacket onto the straw in the middle of the hut. The bride and groom stepped onto it. Without raising his head, Kuzma took the icon from Smallholder's hands, and it became so quiet that the whistling breathing of the curious little boy with the big head could be heard. The bride and groom dropped to their knees at once and bowed at Kuzma's feet. They got up and dropped down again. Kuzma glanced at the bride, and in their eyes, which met for an instant, there was a flash of horror. Kuzma turned pale and thought in horror: "I'll throw the icon to the floor right now..." But his hands involuntarily made a cross in the air with the icon – and Bride, barely touching it with a kiss, caught his hand too with her lips. He thrust the icon upon somebody to one side, took hold of Bride's head with fatherly pain and tenderness, and, kissing her new, fragrant headscarf, he began crying bitterly. Then, seeing nothing because of the tears, he turned and, pushing people aside, strode into the lobby. The snow-laden wind hit him in the face. The snowed-up doorstep was white in the darkness, the wind was roaring through the roof. And beyond the doorstep an impenetrable blizzard was blowing, and the light falling from the little windows, from the depth of the snowy *zavalinka*, hung in hazy shafts...

The blizzard hadn't died down even by the morning. In the rushing grey murk neither Durnovka, nor the mill on the Ridge were to be seen. At times it would get lighter, at times it would be like dusk. The garden whitened, and its humming merged with the humming of the wind, in which there constantly seemed to be the distant ringing of a bell. From the sharp ridges of the snowdrifts rose a snowy haze. From the porch, on which the sheepdogs sat caked in snow, narrowing their eyes and scenting through the freshness of the blizzard a warm, tasty smell from the chimney of the servants' hut, Kuzma had difficulty making out the dark, misty figures of peasants and horses, the sledges, and the jingling of little bells. A pair of horses was harnessed up for the groom, a single one for the bride. The sledges were covered with pieces of felt from Kazan with black designs on the ends. Those in the procession were belted with sashes of many colours. The women had put on wadded coats and covered their heads with shawls, and they walked towards the sledges cautiously, with tiny little steps, repeating fussily: "Heavens,

131

you can't see a thing!…" Both the coat and the blue dress the bride was wearing had been lifted up and wrapped around her head, and she sat down in her sledge onto just her white underskirt. Her head, dressed with a garland of paper flowers, was bundled up in shawls, large and small. Tears had made her so weak that she saw dark figures in the midst of the blizzard and heard its noise, the sound of talking and the festive ringing of little bells as if in a dream. The horses set back their ears and turned their faces away from the snow-laden wind, while the wind scattered the sounds of talking and shouting, it blinded eyes, it whitened moustaches, beards and hats, and those in the procession had difficulty recognizing one another in the haze and the gloom.

"Ugh, fuck this for a laugh!" muttered Vaska, bending his head, taking the reins and sitting down next to the groom.

And coarsely, indifferently, he shouted into the wind:

"Gentlemen boyars, bless the groom as he goes to collect the bride!"

Someone responded:

"God will bless him…"

And the sleigh bells started whining, the runners started creaking, the snowdrifts they scattered started giving off a snowy haze and swirling, and the swirls, manes and tails were carried off to one side…

But in the village, in the church lodge, where people were warming themselves while waiting for the priest, everyone was choking from the charcoal fumes. The air was filled with fumes in the church too, there were fumes, and it was cold and gloomy because of the blizzard, the low vaults, and the grilles at the little windows. Candles were burning only in the hands of the bride and groom and in the hand of the black-haired priest with the big shoulder blades, who bent down towards the wax-spotted book and read quickly through his glasses. There were puddles over the floor – a lot of snow had been brought in on boots and bast shoes – and the wind blew into people's backs from the doors as they were opened. The priest threw stern glances now at the doors, now at the bride and groom, at their tense figures, ready for anything, and their faces, frozen in obedience and humility, lit up in gold from below by the candles. Out of habit, he pronounced some words with apparent feeling, marking them out with touching supplication, but without any thought at all about either the words, or those to whom they referred.

"O God most pure, creator of all creatures…" he said hurriedly, now lowering, now raising his voice, "Thou didst bless Thy servant Abraham and opened the womb of Sarah… Thou didst give Isaac to Rebecca… Thou didst join Jacob unto Rachel… grant to these Thy servants…"

"Names?" he interrupted himself in a stern whisper, addressing the sexton without altering his facial expression. And catching the reply: "Denis, Avdotya…" he continued with feeling:

"Grant to these Thy servants Denis and Yevdokia a peaceful and long life, chastity… that they may see their children's children… and give them of the dew of heaven from on high… fill their houses with wheat, wine and oil… Exalt them like the cedars of Lebanon…"

But those around him, even if they had been listening and had understood him, would still have been thinking of the house of Grey, and not of Abraham and Isaac, and of Deniska, not of a cedar of Lebanon. Deniska himself, short-legged, wearing another man's boots and another man's *poddyovka*, felt awkward and frightened keeping the wedding crown on his motionless head – a huge, copper crown with a cross at the top, which fitted low down on his ears. And the hand of Bride, who seemed even more beautiful and deathly in the crown, was trembling, and the wax of the melting candle was dripping onto the frills of her pale-blue dress…

The blizzard was even more terrible in the dusk. And the horses were driven home especially fast, and Red Vanka's loud-mouthed wife stood in the first sledge and danced like a shaman, waved a handkerchief and yelled into the wind, into the wild, dark murk, into the snow that flew onto her lips and muffled her lupine voice:

The blue-grey dove
Has a golden head…

Moscow
1909–10

133

Note on the Text

This translation of *The Village* has been made from the last Russian edition published in Bunin's lifetime in *Sobranie sochinenii I.A. Bunina* (Berlin: Petropolis, 1934), volume II, pp. 15–190.

Notes

p. 4, *five versts*: A *verst* was a Russian measure of length approximately equivalent to a kilometre.

p. 4, *a "taxable" store*: the Russian government imposed taxes on various goods, including sugar, tobacco, paraffin and matches.

p. 5, *like some bukhara from Emir*: She means "like some emir from Bukhara" – this is the first of numerous instances in the text of characters garbling words and phrases.

p. 8, *kosovorotka*: A man's collarless shirt fastening to one side of the neck.

p. 9, *Peter and Paul's Day*: Celebrated on 29th June (12th July in the New Style calendar).

p. 9, *chuika*: A man's knee-length cloth jacket worn as an outer garment.

p. 10, *poddyovkas*: A *poddyovka* was a man's light, tight-fitting jacket worn beneath an outer coat.

p. 11, *kvas*: A fermented, low-alcohol drink made from rye flour or bread with malt.

p. 11, *arshin*: A Russian measure of length equivalent to approximately seventy centimetres.

p. 12, *zavalinkas*: A *zavalinka* was a mound of earth around the walls of a peasant's hut, serving as protection from the elements and as an informal seat.

p. 13, *Collegiate Assessor*: The eighth of the fourteen Civil-Service ranks in the Table of Ranks introduced by Peter the Great.

p. 13, *...raised in incorruption*: See 1 Corinthians 15:42.

p. 17, *desyatins*: A *desyatin* is a Russian measure of land equivalent to approximately a hectare.

p. 23, *Ilya's Day*: Celebrated on 20th July (2nd August in the New Style calendar).

p. 26, *Come live... bast shoes*: Lines from a song, 'I settled up with my master', about a peasant who tried living in town but could not settle.

p. 28, *imitations of Koltsov and Nikitin*: Alexei Vasilyevich Koltsov (1809–42), the son of a cattle trader, had little formal education and wrote his best poetry in imitation of Russian folk songs; Ivan Savvich Nikitin (1824–61), the son of a shopkeeper, was educated in a seminary for just two years and often wrote of the hardships of impoverished rural and provincial urban life.

p. 29, *the Virgin of Kazan's Day*: Celebrated on 22nd October (4th November in the New Style calendar).

p. 30, *St Michael's Day*: The Archangel Michael is celebrated on 8th November (21st November in the New Style calendar).

p. 33, *armyak*: A peasant's coat of heavy cloth.

p. 36, *chekmen*: A peasant's jacket worn beneath an outer coat.

p. 42, *Tishka... Tikhon Ilyich*: Tishka is the diminutive and Tikhon Ilyich the more formal, respectable name.

p. 45, *Jean-Paul Richter, killed by lightning*: The German writer J.P.F. Richter (1763–1825), known as Jean-Paul, actually died of dropsy.

p. 50, *venderka... vengerka*: Correctly *vengerka*, a short, tight jacket as worn by hussars.

p. 58, *Philaret the Murkyful*: Philaret the Merciful, an eighth-century saint from Asia Minor.

p. 59, *Gattsuk's calendar*: Alexei Alexeyevich Gattsuk (1832–91), archaeologist, publisher and writer, was well-known for his popular church calendar, the first to be published in Russia by a private individual.

p. 61, *Psacs*: The acronym for the Provincial Scholarly Archives Commissions, of which around forty were established from 1884; some thirty of them published periodicals with examples of their work in setting up historical archives at a provincial level.

p. 62, *Smoke*: The novel of 1867 by Ivan Sergeyevich Turgenev (1818–83).

p. 63, *They killed Pushkin... Lermontov... Pisarev... Ryleyev... Dostoevsky... Gogol... Shevchenko... Polezhayev*: All writers who found themselves in conflict in one way or another with the Russian authorities: Alexander Sergeyevich Pushkin (1799–1837) died as the result of a duel thought by some to have been provoked by court circles; Mikhail Yuryevich Lermontov (1814–41) was killed in a duel while in exile in the army in the Caucasus; Dmitry Ivanovich Pisarev (1840–68) was imprisoned for four years for printing radical propaganda before his death from drowning; Kondraty Fyodorovich Ryleyev (1795–1826) was one of five conspirators hanged for their leading roles in the Decembrist revolt of 1825; Fyodor Mikhailovich Dostoevsky (1821–81) was arrested in 1849 for his involvement with a radical circle, then subjected to a mock execution, interrupted by word of reprieve, before Siberian imprisonment; Nikolai Vasilyevich Gogol (1809–52) was driven to death by the physical and psychological strains of his striving for spiritual improvement; Taras Grigorovich Shevchenko (1814–61), the leading Ukrainian writer, spent ten years in exile in Siberia for his radical politics; Alexander Ivanovich Polezhayev (1805–38) was sentenced to serve in the ranks of the army for his liberal and atheistic poetry.

p. 63, *Platon Karatayev*: The peasant who, in Leo Tolstoy's *War and Peace* (1865–69), helps Pierre Bezukhov to find the good in life through simplicity and naturalness.

p. 63, *Yeroshka... Lukashka... Razuvayev... Kolupayev... Salty-chikha... Karamazov... Oblomov... Khlestakov... Nozdryov*: Unflattering examples of the Russian character, all but one taken from literature. Yeroshka and Lukashka are morally dubious Cossacks in Tolstoy's *The Cossacks* (1863); Razuvayev and Kolupayev are unscrupulous accumulators of wealth in the cycle of sketches by Saltykov-Schedrin *The Refuge Monrepos* (1878–79); Darya Nikolayevna Saltykova (1730–1801), nicknamed Saltychikha, was a landowner infamous for her sadistic treatment of her serfs, of whom she murdered well over a hundred; Fyodor Karamazov is the odious father, murdered in Dostoevsky's *The Karamazov Brothers* (1879–80); Ilya Oblomov is the incurably indolent eponymous hero of the novel of 1859 by Ivan Alexandrovich Goncharov (1812–91); Ivan Khlestakov is the vulgar minor official mistaken for a government inspector in Gogol's play of that name (1836); Nozdryov is a lying, cheating landowner in Gogol's *Dead Souls* (1842).

p. 64, *Belinsky*: Vissarion Grigoryevich Belinsky (1811–48), a highly influential radical critic and political thinker.

p. 64, *Saltykov's dying*: Mikhail Yevgrafovich Saltykov (1826–89), who wrote under the pseudonym N. Schedrin and is thus often referred to as "Saltykov-Schedrin", was a civil servant, publicist, novelist and the leading Russian satirist of his time.

p. 66, *Confession or the Gospels*: Leo Tolstoy (1828–1910) wrote his *Confession* in 1879–82, and also made his own translation, with commentaries, of the gospels in 1880–81.

p. 66, *in the Caucasus with the Dukhobors*: Members of a pacifist sect that denied both secular and clerical authority, as well as church ritual, who were forcibly resettled to the Caucasus and Transcaucasia under Nicholas I and were subsequently joined there voluntarily by others; their views elicited the interest and support of Tolstoy.

p. 67, *Prince Vladimir*: Prince Vladimir I of Kiev (*c*.958–1015).

p. 67, *Prince Yaroslav's sarcophagus*: Prince Yaroslav the Wise (*c*.978–1054).

p. 70, *Muromtsev had given the Prime Minister a ticking-off*: Sergei Andreyevich Muromtsev (1850–1910) was Chairman of the First State Duma in 1906.

p. 71, *"Rus, Rus! Where are you rushing to?" Gogol's exclamation*: An inaccurate quotation from the closing lines of Part One of Gogol's *Dead Souls*.

p. 72, *about the minister Durnovo*: Pyotr Nikolayevich Durnovo (1845–1915), Minister of the Interior in 1905.

p. 72, *to frighten the Japanese at Portsmouth, "Vitya" had ordered his suitcases to be packed*: "Vitya" is a Russified version of the surname of Sergei Yulyevich Witte (1849–1915), who headed the Russian delegation in the peace talks with Japan held in Portsmouth, New Hampshire in 1905.

p. 73, *Chernyayev, a fat castrate*: The castrates (*skoptsy*) were a heretical Russian sect.

p. 75, *Makarov's alive*: Admiral Stepan Osipovich Makarov (1849–1904) was killed when his ship struck a Japanese mine, but only his coat was recovered.

p. 95, *The poem 'Who is He?'*: A poem of 1841 about Peter the Great by Apollon Nikolayevich Maikov (1821–97), which featured in many popular anthologies.

p. 96, *two sazhen-high screens*: A *sazhen* was a Russian measure of length equivalent to approximately two metres.

p. 99, *artel*: A cooperative organization of skilled workers.

p. 99, *a pood*: A Russian unit of weight equivalent to approximately sixteen kilograms.

p. 105, *Dreyfus on Devil's Island*: Alfred Dreyfus (1859–1935) was an Alsace-born Jew who in 1893–94, when serving in the French army, was falsely accused and found guilty of passing French secrets to the Germans, and was transported to the penal colony of Devil's Island, causing a national and international scandal.

p. 113, *Flor and Lavr's Day*: The patron saints of domestic animals, and especially horses, were celebrated on 18th August (31st August in the New Style calendar).

p. 122, *So fine like an andel from heaven, like a deman so artful and bad...*: A semi-literate rendition of lines from Lermontov's 'Tamara' (1841), one of a number of his poems regularly included in popular songbooks.

p. 125, *I weep and I wail... kings and beggars...*: Passages from the Order for the Burial of the Dead (Laymen) in the Book of Needs.

p. 130, *a half-shtof*: A *shtof* was a Russian unit of liquid measure equivalent to approximately 1.25 litres.

Extra Material

on

Ivan Bunin's

The Village

Ivan Bunin's Life

Ivan Alexeyevich Bunin was born in the city of Voronezh, in south-western Russia, on 10th October 1870. His father Alexei Nikolayevich, a landowner with property in the Oryol and Tula Provinces, was a descendant of an aristocratic family, that could trace its line back to the fifteenth century. A gifted but impractical man, who was prone to occasional bouts of drinking and gambling, he lost all of his estates, one after another, and ended up destitute when Bunin was a young man. Alexei and his wife Lyudmila Alexandrovna (née Chubarova, also an aristocrat) had nine children, four of whom survived infancy. Bunin had two older brothers, Yuli and Yevgeny, and a younger sister called Maria.

Birth, Background and Education

In an attempt to break Alexei's bad habits and to reduce living expenses, in 1874 the family moved from Voronezh to their estate in Butyrki in the Yelets region of the Oryol Province, some 130 km north of Voronezh. This is where Bunin remained until 1881, tutored privately by Nikolai Osipovich Romashkov, a talented amateur artist and musician, who had studied at the Lazarev Institute of Oriental Languages in Moscow and at Moscow University. Under Romashkov's influence, Bunin contemplated becoming an artist too. Romashkov taught his pupil to read and write using Russian translations of Homer's *Odyssey* and Cervantes's *Don Quixote*. One of the first books Bunin read – an anthology of English poetry from Chaucer to Tennyson, in Russian translation, edited by Nikolai Gerbel (*Angliiskie poety v biografiiakh i obraztsakh*, 1875) – inspired him to become a poet. Spending a great deal of time outdoors, and in close contact with servants and peasants, fostered Bunin's love of nature and detailed knowledge of rural life.

In August 1881, Bunin entered a school in Yelets, where he had to stay, mostly in rented accommodation, for four and a half years, going back to Butyrki for vacations (and, from spring 1883, to the village of Ozerki in the same region, where the family relocated to take possession of an inheritance). Bunin was not a particularly diligent student: he had to repeat his third year because he had failed maths, and was permanently excluded in March 1886 for non-attendance. He preferred to study at home with his brother Yuli, a member of the Populist "Black Repartition" group, who was taken into custody in September 1884 for revolutionary activity and eventually sentenced to a three-year detention at his parents' estate in 1885.

Early Writings and Publications   While in Ozerki, in 1886–87 Bunin wrote his first novel, *Attraction* (*Uvlechenie*), and the first part of the long poem *Pyotr Rogachev* (an imitation of Pushkin's *Eugene Onegin*) – but these did not appear in print in Bunin's lifetime. His first publication, in the St Petersburg weekly *Rodina* (*Motherland*) of 22nd February 1887, was a poem commemorating the untimely death of Semyon Nadson, a fashionable civic poet. Bunin must have been embarrassed by the rather clichéd rhetoric of the piece, because he later claimed that he had made his literary debut with a poem called 'The Village Beggar' (in *Rodina*, 17th May 1887), an emotive snapshot of an old vagabond. In the course of 1888, more of Bunin's poems came out in the St Petersburg literary monthly *Knizhki "Nedeli"* (book supplements to *The Weekly*), run by liberal Populists. His contributions to various periodicals led to a job offer as a staff writer and copy editor at the regional newspaper *Orlovskii vestnik* (*The Oryol Herald*), which he accepted in the autumn of 1889. Subsequently, *Orlovskii vestnik* issued Bunin's first book (a collection of poems written in 1887–91) and printed a number of his stories (most notably 'Small Landowners' in 1891, a series of satirical sketches of Gogolesque types in and around Yelets, with Romashkov serving as a model for the character of Yakov Matveyev). However, Bunin engaged in fiction-writing in earnest only in Poltava, where he moved in late August 1892, following his brother Yuli, to become a local administration employee.

Varvara Pashchenko   Bunin came to Poltava with Varvara Paschenko, the daughter of a Yelets physician. They met when she was a proofreader for *Orlovskii vestnik*, and lived as an unmarried couple, against the will of her parents who feared that Bunin would not be capable of earning a stable income. In Poltava, Bunin worked as a librarian and a statistician and contributed regularly to the newspaper *Poltavskie gubernskie vedomosti* (*The Poltava Regional News*) – as well as, occasionally, to the periodicals in the capital, including prestigious magazines such as *Vestnik Evropy* (*The European Herald*) and *Russkoe bogatstvo* (*The Russian Wealth*). He also joined the Tolstoyans and tried to disseminate the output of their publishing house Posrednik (The Intermediary). He was arrested for doing so without a licence, and sentenced to three months' imprisonment, but was amnestied before he could serve the time, following the death of Alexander III in October 1894 and Nicholas II's accession to the throne. Bunin's ambivalent view of the Tolstoyans is reflected in his later story 'At the Summer House' (1896). That same year, Paschenko ended her turbulent relationship with Bunin, to marry his wealthy friend Arseny Bibikov. In January 1895, Bunin left Poltava for St Petersburg and Moscow to pursue the career of a freelance writer.

On arrival, Bunin became acquainted with representatives *Literary Recognition* of the four most important Russian literary generations, such as the doyen of the Russian realist school Dmitry Grigorovich, the Populist novelists Nikolai Zlatovratsky and Alexander Ertel, as well as Anton Chekhov and the Symbolist poets Konstantin Balmont and Valery Bryusov. Although Bunin strove to maintain independence and impartiality, and did not wish to join any literary camp in particular, he felt more attracted by the classical Russian tradition than by its decadent modernist counterpart (although in 1901 he did bring out his *Falling Leaves* (*Listopad*) poetry collection in the Symbolist publishing house Skorpion). In St Petersburg Bunin published a collection of short stories, *To the End of the World* (*Na krai sveta*, 1897), the title piece describing Ukrainian peasant settlers on their way to the Russian Far East; in Moscow, yet another book of poetry, entitled *Under the Open Sky* (*Pod otkrytym nebom*, 1898); and in 1896 in Oryol, as a supplement to *Orlovskii vestnik*, his translation of *The Song of Hiawatha* by Henry Wadsworth Longfellow, awarded a Pushkin Prize by the Russian Academy of Sciences in 1903. Bunin had taught himself English and, among other things, also translated Byron's *Cain* and Tennyson's 'Godiva' – which, together with Bunin's 1903–07 collections of original poetry, received yet another Pushkin Prize in 1909.

Bunin became a member of the "Wednesday" literary circle, founded in 1898 by the author Nikolai Teleshov, with Zlatovratsky, Chekhov, Alexander Kuprin, Leonid Andreyev and other distinguished authors as its associates. The same year saw the foundation of the publishing cooperative Znanie (Knowledge) – closely linked to Maxim Gorky, whom Bunin met through Chekhov in 1899 – which produced the first five volumes of the first edition of Bunin's collected works (1902–09). In this period, Bunin was invited to undertake several editorial commissions: in 1904–05, he oversaw publications of fiction and poetry in the *Pravda* (*Truth*) magazine, but left its editorial board because of his rift with the Social Democrats on it; in 1907, he was briefly involved in the editing of the *Zemlia* (*Earth*) anthologies; and in 1909, he worked as a literary editor on the magazine *Severnoe siianie* (*Northern Lights*). Meanwhile, his reputation had grown to such an extent that in autumn 1909 he was elected one of the twelve honorary members of the Russian Academy of Sciences in the belles-lettres category. In his capacity as an honorary academician, Bunin was asked to appraise fiction and poetry submitted for the Academy's annual competitions, and his negative peer review of four books of poetry by the modernist Sergei Gorodetsky earned Bunin the Academy's Golden Pushkin Medal for 1911. In 1912, Bunin became an honorary member of the Society of Lovers of Russian Literature (affiliated to Moscow University); he also acted as the Society's sometime Deputy Chair and temporary Chair. On 27th–29th October 1912, the twenty-fifth anniversary of Bunin's literary activity was celebrated at a number of special ceremonies in Moscow, and in 1915, his complete works in six volumes were issued by the publisher Adolf Marx.

Travels and First Marriage Throughout these years of literary endeavour and success, Bunin always found time to travel widely. In autumn 1888 Yuli left Ozerki for the city of Kharkov in Ukraine to take up a job as a statistician. Early the next year, Bunin visited him there, and then went on to the Crimean peninsular to see the cities of Yalta and Sebastopol, thus making his first long-distance trip. From then on, Bunin tried to use every opportunity to travel, the further the better; a sedentary lifestyle had never been quite for him, especially in his younger years. His attempt to settle down in Odessa (a large port on the Black Sea) and marry, on 23rd September 1898, Anna Tsakni

– the daughter of the publisher of the newspaper *Iuzhnoe obozrenie* (*Southern Review*), which Bunin wrote for – ended in a separation in early March 1900. Bunin and Tsakni had a son, Nikolai, who was born in August 1900 and died in January 1905 of complications caused by scarlet fever and measles.

This failed marriage led to a period of increased travel. In October and November 1900, Bunin went abroad for the first time with his friend Vladimir Kurovsky, an artist and custodian of the Odessa Art Museum. They visited Germany, France, Austria and Switzerland. In April 1903, Bunin went to Istanbul, which led to a lifelong fascination with the city (afterwards, Bunin returned to it at least twelve times). From late December 1903 to early February 1904, he travelled through France and Italy in the company of the playwright Sergei Naidyonov. Four months later, Bunin toured the Caucasus and in July 1905 he went to Finland (then part of the Russian Empire).

In November 1905 Bunin began a relationship with his fu- *Second Marriage* ture second wife, Vera Nikolayevna Muromtseva, a graduate of the Science Faculty of the Higher Courses for Women in Moscow and the niece of a State Duma chairman. They started living together soon afterwards, but married only in November 1922 in Paris (as Bunin's divorce from Tsakni was finalized on 20th June 1922). She accompanied him on his travels, which were again frequent and far-ranging. In April and May 1907, Bunin and Muromtseva journeyed to Egypt, Syria and Palestine, via Turkey and Greece – a trip that few Russians at the time ever considered making (it was described in the *Temple of the Sun* cycle, 1907–11). Then, in March and April 1909, Bunin and Muromtseva went to Italy (via Austria), spending much of their time on the Italian island of Capri, later described in Bunin's story 'The Gentleman from San Francisco' (1915), and between March and May 1910, they went to Algiers and Tunisia – via Austria, Italy, France, Greece and Turkey – and paid a visit to the Sahara desert. Between December 1910 and April 1911, the couple returned to Egypt, and from there journeyed to Ceylon (now Sri Lanka). They even contemplated going from Ceylon to Japan, but ran out of time and money. Bunin's diary of the voyage along the Suez Canal and across the Red Sea and the Indian Ocean was published in 1925–26 under the title *The Waters Are Many*;

in addition, Ceylon served as a background for his 1914 story 'Brothers', and one of its ancient capitals, Anuradhapura, was depicted in the 1924 story 'The City of the King of Kings'.

Bunin's journeys to remote exotic destinations assisted him in acquiring an enhanced awareness of Muslim, Jewish and Buddhist traditions, uncommon in a Russian intellectual with a strong Orthodox Christian background. Examples of this insight can be found for instance in his poems 'Mohammed in Exile' (1906), 'Torah' (1914) and the short stories 'Gautami' (1919) and 'The Night of Renunciation' (1921). Between November 1911 and March 1914, Bunin and Muromtseva returned to Italy several times (mostly to Capri), and visited Germany, Austria, Switzerland and Greece on their way to and from Russia. Bunin also went on a Black Sea voyage with his brother Yuli in summer 1913, stopping in Batumi, Trabzon, Istanbul and Constanta, and then proceeding to Bucharest, Iasi and Chişinău – Bunin later used a Bessarabian setting for his 1916 story 'A Song about a Noble Brigand'. A year later, the brothers made a trip along the Volga river, from Saratov to Yaroslavl. They were in Samara when the news about the assassination of Archduke Franz Ferdinand in Sarajevo reached them.

First World War,
Russian Revolution and
Emigration

After war was declared, Bunin spent three months doing little else besides reading newspapers in a state of shock. On 28th September 1914, the *Russkoe slovo* (*Russian Word*) periodical published his protest against German atrocities, written on behalf of Russian authors, actors and artists. In it, Bunin claimed that German soldiers were reminding mankind that "the ancient beast inside the human being is alive and strong, and even the nations that are leading the advance of civilization can easily give evil will a free rein and become like the half-naked hordes of their ancestors, who crushed the legacy of the classical world under their heavy feet fifteen centuries ago". However, the war did not make Bunin a chauvinist ascribing good and evil qualities to particular nations; on the contrary, he believed that the epoch ushered in by the war might well be dominated by a killer of indeterminate (or any) nationality, capable of executing defenceless people for no reason and without remorse – this is illustrated by the character of Adam Sokolovich in his 1916 story 'Loopy Ears', openly polemical against Dostoevsky's *Crime and Punishment* and its repentant murderer Raskolnikov. The ensuing February and October 1917 revolutions confirmed Bunin's worst fears, harboured at least since the Russian civil unrest of 1905–07, which he witnessed in Odessa (the Jewish pogroms in September and October 1905), Moscow (the December 1905 uprising) and in the countryside (where, in June 1906, peasants set the estates of Bunin's brother Yevgeny and cousin Sofia Pusheshnikova on fire).

Bunin was in Moscow when the February 1917 Revolution took place. Although a man of moderate left-wing persuasions and by no means a monarchist, Bunin dismissed the Provisional Government as a "travesty". In early April 1917, he ended his long-term friendship with Gorky over his proximity to the Bolsheviks, whose coup d'état forced the Bunins out of Moscow. On 21st May 1918, they left for Odessa, which at the time belonged to the independent state of Ukraine, with Hetman Pavlo Skoropadsky as its head. They arrived on 3rd June, via Orsha, Minsk, Gomel and Kiev, and remained in Odessa for almost twenty months, surviving the rule of the Ukrainian Directorate in November and December 1918, the French occupation from December 1918 to April 1919, the Bolshevik regime of April to August 1919 and the White (Volunteer) Army administration of August 1919 to early 1920. In his diary *Cursed Days* (*Okaiannye dni*, 1936), covering life in Bolshevik-controlled Moscow and Odessa, Bunin noted: "Our children and grandchildren won't be able even to imagine the Russia that we once (only yesterday) lived in – Russia with all its might, complexity, wealth and happiness, which we neither appreciated nor understood." In Odessa, Bunin contributed to local periodicals, such as *Odesskie novosti* (*Odessa News*), *Odesskii listok* (*Odessa Sheet*) and *Nashe slovo* (*Our Word*), as well as co-editing the newspaper *Iuzhnoe slovo* (*Word of the South*), set up by the Volunteer Army. On 26th January 1920, facing the danger of yet another Bolshevik takeover, Bunin (who had by now become an accomplished anti-communist) and Muromtseva left Russia for good. Their journey to Istanbul on the Sparta steamship is described in the story 'The End' (1921).

The couple settled in France, arriving there on 28th March 1920, via Sofia and Belgrade. From 1923, a pattern was established, according to which the Bunins tended to spend the winter months in Paris, and spring, summer and autumn at various villas on the French Riviera, most frequently in the town of Grasse. Bunin's royalties for translations into foreign languages and for publications in the Russian émigré press

147

– for example the Parisian newspapers *Poslednie novosti* (*The Latest News*), *Vozrozhdenie* (*Revival*) and *Rossiia i slavianstvo* (*Russia and the Slavic World*) – augmented by a grant from the Czechoslovakian government (disbursed in 1924–28), allowed him not only to lead a modestly independent life, but also to take under his wing a number of young aspiring Russian authors, who were often invited to stay for lengthy periods of time under one roof with the Bunins. Of these authors, Galina Kuznetsova was Bunin's lover between 1926 and 1934 (when she left him for the singer Margarita Stepun), and Leonid Zurov eventually inherited Bunin's intellectual property rights and archive.

Bunin's attitude to Russia differed from that of a typical émigré by avoiding cheap sentimentality and futile vindictiveness. In his story 'Eternal Spring' (1923), Bunin depicted pre-revolutionary Russia as a remote museum-like past, a return to which was neither possible nor desirable. Perhaps he was aided in this attitude by being something of a citizen of the world, who only felt at home when he was on the move. Even as a stateless person, Bunin managed to go abroad (e.g. to Wiesbaden from July to September 1921 and to London in February 1925), undeterred by significant visa problems. In his new poetry and fiction, Russian history and culture remained only one of many different themes. Still, his magnum opus, the loosely autobiographical novel *Arsenyev's Life* (*Zhizn' Arsen'eva*, written between 1927 and 1938 and first published in full in 1952), focused on a meticulous recreation of everyday existence in provincial Russia in the 1870s–90s.

In 1933, after years of vigorous campaigning behind the scenes, Bunin received the Nobel Prize for Literature, "for the strict artistry with which he has carried on the classical Russian traditions in prose writing" (the Swedish Academy's decision of 9th November). He was the first Russian to achieve this distinction. In December that year, accompanied by both Muromtseva and Kuznetsova, he travelled to Stockholm to the award ceremony. A large proportion of the prize money, around 120,000 French francs, was given away by Bunin to various charitable causes in support of Russian émigré circles. In 1934–39, the Berlin-based Petropolis publishing house issued a revised edition of Bunin's collected works in Russian, in twelve volumes. On publishing business, and to give a series of public readings (at which he excelled as a gifted orator), Bunin visited Brussels, London, Czechoslovakia, Germany, Italy, Yugoslavia, Lithuania,

Latvia and Estonia between 1935 and 1938. However, the life of a minor celebrity was not devoid of humiliating moments. Bunin was briefly detained by the German border guards in Lindau on 27th October 1936 for overstaying his visa (see the note "Russian Exile's Protest: Alleged Brutality at German Customs" in *The Times* of 3rd November 1936).

From September 1939 until May 1945, the Bunins had to re- *The Second World War* main in Grasse uninterruptedly. In these years of isolation and *and the Final Years* despair, Bunin wrote his finest short stories, which comprised the 1946 *Dark Avenues* (*Temnye allei*) collection. Although living in poverty, he firmly declined invitations to contribute to the collaborationist press, and gave shelter to Jews (e.g. the essayist Alexander Bakhrakh and the pianist Alexander Lieberman) who were hiding from the Nazis. After the war, the Bunins returned to Paris. Bunin's deteriorating health (he suffered from emphysema and underwent prostate surgery on 4th September 1950) and difficult financial circumstances (in 1949–51, he even accepted a monthly allowance of 10,000 francs from the millionaire and philanthropist Solomon Atran) did not present much opportunity for travel, although he allowed himself several stays in a Russian guesthouse in Juan-les-Pins between 1947 and 1949. The seventy-fifth and eightieth anniversaries of Bunin's birth were used to collect donations for his financial support. He rejected Soviet attempts to lure him back to Russia (partly prompted by the friend and author Alexei Tolstoy's letter to Stalin of 17th June 1941 about Bunin's miserable existence in war-torn France), and stopped a collection of his works, in preparation by a state publishing house in Moscow, from publication, because he could not exercise control over its content. On the other hand, in late 1947 he left the Union of Russian Writers and Journalists in France (which he used to chair), after it had expelled those of its members who had taken Soviet passports in the aftermath of a 1946 Supreme Soviet decree returning citizenship rights to former subjects of the Russian Empire. As a result, he fell out with his old friend and sponsor Maria Tsetlina, whose late husband was an heir to the Wissotzky Tea company. Bunin's controversial *Memoirs* (*Vospominaniia*, 1950), which pulled no punches in challenging the reputations of famous Russians such as Gorky and the futurist poet Vladimir Mayakovsky, was his last completed large-scale project. He died on 8th November 1953, of pneumonia, while

149

working on a book called *About Chekhov* (*O Chekhove*), intended to commemorate the fiftieth anniversary of his death. Its unfinished manuscript, edited by Muromtseva and Zurov, appeared posthumously, in 1955.

Ivan Bunin's Works

Genre   Bunin began his literary career as a poet specializing in rather detached sketches of characters and locations, memorable for either their typicality or exoticism. His poetic style, earning him a reputation as "the only significant poet of the Symbolist age who was not a Symbolist" (Georgette Donchin in *The Times Literary Supplement* of 10th May 1957), owes a great deal to realistic landscape and portrait painting. Bunin found it impossible to separate his poetry from his prose, regularly publishing both under the same cover. His trademark "unnarrative" (D.S. Mirsky) atmospheric prose often reads like poetry – such as the story 'Antonov Apples' (*Antonovskie iabloki*, 1900) – in which the smell of apples evokes a picture of the disappearing lifestyle of landowners in the south-west of Russia, accompanied by striking images of nature in the autumn. In a conversation with his nephew Nikolai Pusheshnikov, Bunin admitted that, for him, the key to a successful story was "finding the right sound. As soon as I have found it, the rest practically writes itself... But I never write what I want the way I want it. I don't dare. I would prefer to avoid any form and ignore literary devices". Thus, Bunin felt obliged to make certain concessions to conventional public taste, and framed his momentary observations of human types, moods, events and nature scenes into various traditional generic structures. Many of his short stories are in fact poems in prose, and the prose genre most befitting his idiosyncratic manner is perhaps that of a diary (often reworked for publication). Still, even his more substantial prose pieces, such as the 25,000-word novella *Dry Valley* (*Sukhodol*, 1911) – about the decline of a gentry family, told from a female servant's point of view – were called "poems" or "prose poems" by the critics, and it was Bunin's "lyrical prose style [that] provided a welcome contrast with the rather colourless naturalism of the most influential group of novelists in Russia" (R.D. Charques in *The Times Literary Supplement* of 7th March 1935).

Bunin's lyricism, however, does not translate into idealiza- *The Village* tion of his favourite subject, rural Russia, but rather offsets its mercilessly truthful representation, frequently making it appear even bleaker than it would have done otherwise. His first large-scale prose work, *The Village* (*Derevnia*, 1910), is a good example of this. It is a story of two ageing peasant brothers, Tikhon and Kuzma, an owner and a manager of an estate tellingly named Durnovka (derived from a Russian word for "bad" or "evil"). The hard-working Tikhon, preoccupied almost solely with material gain, and the dreamer Kuzma, an undistinguished poet without a stable occupation, epitomize two extremes of the Russian national character. Durnovka is not easy to manage, because its inhabitants – personified by the needy peasant Grey and his son Deniska – are lazy drunks, indulging in domestic violence and wanton unruliness, and living in conditions of "almost incredible ignorance, hate, poverty, dirt, cruelty, idleness, supineness" (Harold Hannyngton Child in *The Times Literary Supplement* of 25th October 1923). Neither of the brothers has anybody to bequeath Durnovka to, and they decide to sell it and to move to a nearby town. *The Village* – a symbol of Russia in its entirety, displaying Chekhov's influence in its descriptions of the steppe and a cherry orchard – was not intended "as an indictment of the peasant class. No class depicted in the book has any redeeming feature, and the whole picture of pre-revolutionary provincial life is painted in the blackest possible tones" (Georgette Donchin).

Bunin's perception of the West hardly provides any alter- *The Gentleman from* native. The Tolstoyan theme of the uselessness of material *San Francisco* wealth in the face of looming death, obvious in *The Village*, is developed further in 'The Gentleman from San Francisco', Bunin's most famous short story, written with "the intensity of an apocalyptic vision of the horror and falsity of modern civilization" (John Middleton Murry in *The Times Literary Supplement* of 20th April 1922). In the story, Western civilization is symbolized by an ocean liner, suggestively called *Atlantis*, which conveys a holidaying American millionaire and his family from the United States to Europe, and shortly afterwards carries his corpse in the opposite direction (he dies suddenly of a heart attack). The stokers in the engine room are endlessly toiling to ensure that the well-to-do passengers upstairs can enjoy a life of exquisite luxury, and the unswerving progress of this sophisticated piece of machinery is supervised by a captain who looks like a heathen idol. It is hard not to become "fascinated by this grandiose vision of the magnificence, the immense technical accomplishment of the setting man has made for himself, and by this ruthless vision of the shrivelled, inhuman, unclean thing that cowers within it", wrote *The Times* of 17th May 1922.

Bunin's concept of the East does not offer much consolation either. Thus, denizens of the lost Paradise – the island of Ceylon – succumb too easily to the fatal temptation of pursuing sensual pleasures, which should have been renounced in compliance with Buddhist teachings. For this, Bunin partly blames the corrupting influence of the exploitative West (see for example the young rickshaw man in 'Brothers', who commits suicide because his beloved becomes a rich westerner's concubine). However, his insufficiently profound knowledge of both Eastern and Western ways appears to let him down on more than one occasion and undermine the value of the didactic message of his tales. ("Was ever an American citizen on board a liner in the Mediterranean seen to wear a silk top hat, patent-leather shoes and spats? And if in Ceylon the English officers drive the rickshaw men till they 'hear the death rattle in their throats', then a great number of people must have conspired together to misrepresent to us the facts of life upon that island," noted Cyril Bentham Falls in *The Times Literary Supplement* of 6th March 1924.) In this context, it is hardly surprising that John Middleton Murry said of Bunin: "If his West is a nightmare, his East is a dream – and we are left to wander uneasily between the two." Besides, it has to be admitted that Bunin's East, with its abject poverty, idolization of deities and oppressively hot summer nights, looks too much like Russia at times (see the 1916 story 'The Compatriot'). This might be partly explained by Bunin's conviction, acquired after travelling far and wide, that people are similar wherever one goes. The jobless, alcoholic sea captain in the story 'Chang's Dreams' (*Sny Changa*, 1916) seems to express Bunin's own pessimistic view of human nature when he says: "I've been across the entire globe. Life is the same everywhere!... People have neither God, nor conscience, nor any practical goal in life, nor love, nor friendship, nor honesty – not even simple pity."

Arsenyev's Life   Yet, perhaps paradoxically, Bunin's works continue to display his appreciation of every moment of his existence – no matter how dark – and his gratitude for being able to observe, remember and portray anything remarkable – even seemingly insignificant occurrences, which might never be repeated and are therefore uniquely precious. A selection of such moments, united by one lifespan, forms the basis of his longest work, the autobiographical novel *Arsenyev's Life* (the first four parts of which were translated into English in 1933 as *The Well of Days*). In it, Bunin's memory is cast back to the times of his childhood and youth, to follow the pattern established in Russia by Leo Tolstoy's 1852–56 autobiographical trilogy *Childhood, Boyhood, Youth*. The first part tells Arsenyev's story from his birth on a family estate to his first year at school in the nearest town; the second ends with his decision to leave the school while in his fifth year and remain on the estate; the third describes the loss of his virginity at the age of seventeen and an affair with a young married peasant woman; and the fourth his departure from the family estate for Kharkov, his travels through the south of Russia and, when in Oryol, his acquaintance with a woman called Lika (a character loosely modelled on Varvara Paschenko), who will soon become his lover and companion. The narrative pace is deliberately slow, bringing together what appears to be a series of brilliantly executed miniature paintings (Bunin himself compared his creative method to an old photographic album). Although Arsenyev's life is not particularly eventful, the reader is amply compensated for the paucity of action by "the magical freshness and fullness of the feelings and emotions of youth [that] are blended throughout with a special poetical sense for landscape and great depth of passionate receptivity" (Edward Garnett in *The Manchester Guardian* of 7th April 1933). The fourth part concludes with the depiction of a funeral train at the Oryol railway station, carrying the body of the Grand Duke Nikolai Nikolayevich Sr, who died in the Crimea in 1891. His son, Nikolai Nikolayevich Jr, is portrayed coming off the train, but the next scene, as if in a cinematic "flash forward", suddenly describes Nikolai Nikolayevich Jr himself lying in state in Antibes (Bunin visited his villa there shortly before the funeral). The death of this last undisputed heir to the Russian throne in 1929, quite out of place in a family chronicle set in the 1870s–90s, symbolizes the death of old Russia (to which *Arsenyev's Life* serves as an epitaph), and also gives the reader an early indication of more tragedies to come, including Lika's untimely demise in the fifth part of the novel (written much later and dealing, *inter alia*, with Arsenyev's attempts to find his own voice as an author).

In a review of *The Well of Days*, dated 21st March 1933, a London *Times* critic claimed that the book was "shadowed by the sense of mortality which is almost always present in Ivan Bunin's work". It appears that in *Arsenyev's Life*, Bunin feels nostalgic about the Russia of his youth not so much because the Bolsheviks have taken over the country and have changed it beyond recognition, but because his detailed memories of it, which he carries inside him, are bound to disappear when he dies.

The Liberation of Tolstoy   It was this apprehension of mortality that Bunin tried to come to terms with in his next, non-fictional book *The Liberation of Tolstoy* (*Osvobozhdenie Tolstogo*, 1937). Bunin had held Tolstoy in the highest esteem long before they met in January 1894, owing a considerable debt of gratitude to him as an artist (for instance, 'Chang's Dreams', told from a dog's point of view, was undoubtedly inspired by Tolstoy's 'Kholstomer: The Story of a Horse', and 'The Gentleman from San Francisco' by 'The Death of Ivan Ilyich'). For Bunin, Tolstoy was in the same league as Buddha and King Solomon (see his 1925 story 'The Night', also known as 'Cicadas'), and is portrayed by him as a religious teacher who offers people advice on how to cope with death. According to Bunin, Tolstoy teaches that death is a liberation from the constraints of time and space, a return to an eternity which is full of love. By making this claim, Bunin polemicizes against alternative views of Tolstoy, including those of the Italian author Delfino Cinelli, the Russian émigré author Mark Aldanov, the lawyer, politician and diplomat Vasily Maklakov (1869–1957) – and Lenin. Quotations from their works are interspersed with Bunin's and others' personal reminiscences of Tolstoy. The book as a whole is framed by the repetition of phrases (such as, "I lived with Leo Nikolayevich for forty-eight years and I still couldn't understand what he was like", a comment made by Tolstoy's widow Sofia) and episodes (such as Tolstoy asking the zoologist Sergei Usov how long a person can survive if bitten by a mad dog), which function much as rhymes in a poem do, holding the structure together. Bunin's understanding of Tolstoy seems to have been determined, first and foremost, by his own concern with mortality, which throws into sharper relief an admiration of all the things life can offer, including love in all its manifestations.

Already in his 1924 novella *Mitya's Love* (*Mitina liubov'*) – about a student who shoots himself because he cheated on his sweetheart, an aspiring actress, with a married peasant girl, while the actress, in an unrelated chain of events, left him for the headmaster of her drama school, a notorious womanizer – Bunin's "two principal motifs, love and death, the two most wonderful and incomprehensible things in life, meet and intermingle, and are woven into a fabric of unforgettable beauty" (Gleb Struve in *The Observer* of 25th February 1934).

The interaction of these two motifs provided a common ground for most of his stories forming the cycle *Dark Avenues* (*Temnye allei*), written in 1937–45 and published, in different combinations, in the US in 1943 and in France in 1946. Bunin compared this book with Boccaccio's *Decameron*, because it was created at the height of the Nazi plague "to escape to a different world, where there was no bloodshed and people were not burnt alive" (Vera Bunina), but also presumably because it is a veritable encyclopedia of heterosexual relationships, complete with fatal attractions, love at first sight, unforgettable one-night stands, lightning-fast seduction of under-age children and even rape. The book's title refers to a popular garden feature on Russian estates – a setting for many of the stories – but also brings to mind the configuration of female genitalia. In his letter to the satirist Nadezhda Teffi of 23rd February 1944, Bunin stated, however, that the content of the stories "is not at all frivolous, but tragic... and all the stories in the book are only about love, about its 'dark' and, more often than not, gloomy and sinister avenues".

The title story – about a chance encounter between two old lovers, an army officer and an ex-serf, who suddenly reveals that, many years after he left her, she still harbours deep feelings for him – explains that the expression "dark avenues" has been borrowed from an 1842 poem by Nikolai Ogaryov (1813–77) called 'An Ordinary Tale' (*'Obyknovennaia povest'*), in praise of first love (although the two young lovers mentioned in it later go their separate ways). It is true that some stories in the collection may appear either ordinary, or perhaps romantically clichéd, if summarized in terms of their plot alone. There are also stories that would not be out of place in a soap opera. Examples include a wronged husband coming to the Caucasus to look for

155

his wife, who eloped there with her lover, and killing himself when he does not find her ('The Caucasus'); a Georgian man spending a night with a prostitute and killing her accidentally in a fit of passion ('Miss Klara'); an artist's daughter's teenage infatuation with another artist, leading to her suicide ('Galya Ganskaya'); and a woman returning to her old flame after a loveless marriage but dying shortly afterwards, when giving premature birth ('Natalie'). There are also tales of an irresistible passion that bridges the social and the human-animal divides. In 'Tanya', an aristocrat and a servant girl find that their feelings for one another are very serious, only to be separated for ever by the Russian Revolution (this story has invited comparisons between *Dark Avenues* and *Lady Chatterley's Lover* by D.H. Lawrence). In 'Iron Coat', a woman has had sexual intercourse with a bear (this story was apparently influenced by Prosper Mérimée's 'Lokis', 1869).

Dark Avenues could have easily turned out both trite and shockingly lewd. However, Bunin's mastery of language and characterization ensured that he successfully avoided the pitfalls of banality and vulgarity and struck a perfect balance between innocence and eroticism (irrespective of the criticism levelled at him that his upper- and middle-class female characters behave as if they were immoral members of the Young Communist League). As Robin Raleigh-King wrote of *Dark Avenues* in *The Times Literary Supplement* of 6th May 1949, Bunin "pinpoints the essential moments and details of a lifetime with such acid sharpness and such skill that for a moment the real world appears pallid by comparison... 'In Paris', the story of an elderly exile from Russia meeting a charming Russian woman in Paris, is an excellent example of the author's power to infuse nobility, breadth of vision and eternal significance into what might have been an ordinary love affair."

Not only does *Dark Avenues* offer a rare variety of types and situations, but every story in it is written in its own rhythm and style, 'Pure Monday' – about a woman torn between a man she loves and her urge to become a nun – being one of Bunin's best. And, in the words of Robin Raleigh-King, "the dominant note of nearly all these stories is one of regret – regret that life recedes like a tide, regret that one must stand alone on the desolate beach, regret that a human being is only capable of living one full cycle before he dies".

Bunin's *Memoirs*, his last completed book, is a collection *Memoirs* of reminiscences written in 1927–50 and structured as a musical composition, with the opening 'Autobiographical Notes' providing an overture of sorts to introduce various themes, which are elaborated upon in the ensuing sections on the musicians Sergei Rachmaninov and Fyodor Shalyapin, the artist Ilya Repin, the authors Jerome K. Jerome, Chekhov, Leo and Alexei Tolstoy, Alexander Kuprin, Prince Peter of Oldenburg and others. Bunin's memoirs are decidedly literary, filled with quotations from fiction, poetry and literary criticism of diverse provenance, as well as occasional fragments from personal correspondence and reference sources. Some quotations function as leitmotifs, used more than once in the narration (such as those from Maximilian Voloshin's 1906 poem 'The Angel of Vengeance' and Gorky's 1906 essay 'The City of the Yellow Devil'). Bunin's characterization of people he knew is largely affected by his rather conservative aesthetics, in the tradition of classical Russian realism, exemplified by Leo Tolstoy and Chekhov (whose spiritual heir Bunin believed himself to be). His biased view of Gorky, Vladimir Mayakovsky and Alexander Blok "that makes him incapable of perceiving their merit as writers" (R.D. Charques in *The Times Literary Supplement* of 6th April 1951), stems from his conviction that it was their loss of touch with reality, manifested in their modernist writings, that brought them to the Bolshevik camp. The almost forgotten Alexander Ertel seems to embody Bunin's ideal of a man, being both a gifted author and a successful estate manager (i.e. happily embracing a fantasy world and a businesslike attitude); a philanthropist who avoided the extremes of Tolstoyanism and revolutionism; and a self-made man who stayed away from the excesses of larger-than-life characters such as Kuprin and Shalyapin. Yet, as R.D. Charques points out, "the best pages in the book are those on Chekhov", and it was to commemorate the fiftieth anniversary of Chekhov's death that Bunin set to work on his new book *About Chekhov*, which remained unfinished.

The first section of *About Chekhov*, prepared for pub- *About Chekhov* lication in 1955 by Vera Bunina and Zurov, consists of biographical information on Chekhov, Bunin's memories of him (Bunin knew Chekhov's family and was a regular guest in the Chekhov household) and a section on Chekhov's romantic involvement with the author Lydia Avilova. Avilova's letters to

157

the Bunins, written when she was in Czechoslovakia in 1922–24, are also included in the book (just as reminiscences of Leo Tolstoy by the Bunins' friend Ekaterina Lopatina became part of *The Liberation of Tolstoy*). The second section consists of quotations from Chekhov's letters and Bunin's marginalia on the studies of Chekhov's art by the émigré scholar Pyotr Bitsilli and the Soviet critic Vladimir Ermilov, and on a collection of reminiscences about Chekhov with contributions from Teleshov, Gorky, Kuprin and others. In terms of an overarching concept, not much can be gleaned from this compilation of assorted fragments, but it is precisely the book's fragmentary nature that encapsulates the spirit of Bunin's persistent endeavour to capture fleeting impressions and images.

– Andrei Rogatchevski, 2008

Select Bibliography

Biographies and Additional Background Material in Russian:
Bunina, Vera, *Zhizn' Bunina: 1870–1906* (The Life of Bunin; Paris, [s.n.], 1958)

Kuznetsova, Galina, *Grasskii dnevnik* (The Grasse Diary; Washington: Victor Kamkin, 1967)

Grin, Militsa (ed.), *Ustami Buninykh* (As Spoken by the Bunins; Frankfurt/Main: Posev, 1977–82; in 3 vols)

Bakhrakh, Alexander, *Bunin v khalate* (Bunin in a Dressing Gown; Bayville: Tovarishchestvo zarubezhnykh pisatelei, 1979)

Burlaka, D.K. (ed.), *I.A. Bunin: Pro et contra: Lichnost i tvorchestvo Ivana Bunina v otsenke russkikh i zarubezhnykh myslitelei i issledovatelei: Antologiia* (St Petersburg: Izdatel'stvo Russkogo Khristianskogo gumanitarnogo instituta, 2001)

Baboreko, Alexander, *Bunin: Zhizneopisanie* (The Life of Bunin; Moscow: Molodaia gvardiia, 2004)

Biographies and Additional Background Material in English:
Heywood, Anthony J., *Catalogue of the I.A. Bunin, V.N. Bunina, L.F. Zurov and E.M. Lopatina Collections* (Leeds: Leeds University Press, 2000)

Kryzytski, Serge, *The Works of Ivan Bunin* (The Hague: Mouton, 1971)

Woodward, James B., *Ivan Bunin: A Study of His Fiction* (Chapel Hill: University of North Carolina Press, 1980)

Connolly, Julian W., *Ivan Bunin* (Boston, MA: Twayne Publishers, 1982)

Marullo, Thomas Gaiton, (ed.), *Ivan Bunin: Russian Requiem, 1885–1920: A Portrait from Letters, Diaries and Fiction* (Chicago: Ivan R. Dee, 1993)

Marullo, Thomas Gaiton, (ed.), *Ivan Bunin: From the Other Shore, 1920–1933: A Portrait from Letters, Diaries and Fiction* (Chicago: Ivan R. Dee, 1995)

Marullo, Thomas Gaiton, (ed.), *Ivan Bunin: The Twilight of Emigré Russia, 1934–1953: A Portrait from Letters, Diaries and Memoirs* (Chicago: Ivan R. Dee, 2002)

Zweers, Alexander F., *The Narratology of the Autobiography: An Analysis of the Literary Devices Employed in Ivan Bunin's* The Life of Arsen'ev (New York: Peter Lang, 1997)

Appendix

Прадеда Красовых, прозванного на дворне Цыганом, затравил борзыми барин Дурново. Цыган отбил у него, у своего господина, любовницу. Дурново приказал вывести Цыгана в поле, за Дурновку, и посадить на бугре. Сам же выехал со сворой и крикнул: «Ату его!» Цыган, сидевший в оцепенении, кинулся бежать. А бегать от борзых не следует.

Деду Красовых удалось получить вольную. Он ушел с семьей в город — и скоро прославился: стал знаменитым вором. Нанял в Черной Слободе хибарку для жены, посадил ее плести на продажу кружево, а сам, с каким-то мещанином Белокопытовым, поехал по губернии грабить церкви. Когда его поймали, он вел себя так, что им долго восхищались по всему уезду: стоит себе будто бы в плисовом кафтане и в козловых сапожках, нахально играет скулами, глазами и почтительнейше сознается даже в самом малейшем из своих несметных дел:

— Так точно-с. Так точно-с.

А родитель Красовых был мелким шибаем. Ездил по уезду, жил одно время в родной Дурновке, завел было там лавочку, но прогорел, запил, воротился в город и помер. Послужив по лавкам, торгашили и сыновья его, Тихон и Кузьма. Тянутся, бывало, в телеге с рундуком посередке и заунывно орут:

— Ба-абы, това-ару! Ба-абы, това-ару!

Товар — зеркальца, мыльца, перстни, нитки, платки, иголки, крендели — в рундуке. А в телеге все, что добыто в обмен на товар: дохлые кошки, яйца, холсты, тряпки...

Но, проездив несколько лет, братья однажды чуть ножами не порезались — и разошлись от греха. Кузьма нанялся к гуртовщику, Тихон снял постоялый дворишко на шоссе при станции Воргол, верстах в пяти от Дурновки, и открыл кабак и «черную» лавочку: «торговля мелочного товару чаю сахору тобаку сигар и протчего».

Годам к сорока борода Тихона уже кое-где серебрилась. Но красив, высок, строен был он по-прежнему; лицом строг, смугл,

163

чуть-чуть ряб, в плечах широк и сух, в разговоре властен и резок, в движениях быстр и ловок. Только брови стали сдвигаться все чаще да глаза блестеть еще острей, чем прежде.

Неутомимо гонял он за становыми — в те глухие осенние поры, когда взыскивают подати и идут по деревне торги за торгами. Неутомимо скупал у помещиков хлеб на корню, снимал за бесценок землю... Жил он долго с немой кухаркой, — «не плохо, ничего не разбрешет!» — имел от нее ребенка, которого она приспала, задавила во сне, потом женился на пожилой горничной старухи-княжны Шаховой. А женившись, взяв приданого, «доконал» потомка обнищавших Дурново, полного, ласкового барчука, лысого на двадцать пятом году, но с великолепной каштановой бородой. И мужики так и ахнули от гордости, когда взял он дурновское именьице: ведь чуть не вся Дурновка состоит из Красовых!

Ахали они и на то, как это ухитрялся он не разорваться: торговать, покупать, чуть не каждый день бывать в именье, ястребом следить за каждой пядью земли... Ахали и говорили:

— Лют! Зато и хозяин!

Убеждал их в этом и сам Тихон Ильич. Часто наставлял:

— Живем — не мотаем, попадешься — обротаем. Но — по справедливости. Я, брат, человек русский. Мне твоего даром не надо, но имей в виду: своего я тебе трынки не отдам! Баловать, — нет, заметь, не побалую!

А Настасья Петровна (ходившая по-утиному, носками внутрь, переваливаясь, — от постоянной беременности, все кончавшейся мертвыми девочками, — желтая, опухшая, с редкими белесыми волосами) стонала, слушая:

— Ох, и прост же ты, посмотрю я на тебя! Что ты с ним, глупым, трудишься? Ты его уму-разуму учишь, а ему и горя мало. Ишь, ноги-то расставил, — эмирский бухар какой!

Осенью возле постоялого двора, стоявшего одним боком к шоссе, другим к станции и элеватору, стоном стонал скрип колес: обозы с хлебом сворачивали и сверху и снизу. И поминутно визжал блок то на двери в кабак, где отпускала Настасья Петровна, то на двери в лавку, — темную, грязную, крепко пахнущую мылом, сельдями, махоркой, мятным пряником, керосином. И поминутно раздавалось в кабаке:

— У-ух! И здорова́ же водка у тебя, Петровна! Аж в лоб стукнула, пропади она пропадом.

— Сахаром в уста, любезный!

— Либо она у тебя с нюхальным табаком?

— Вот и вышел дураком!

А в лавке было еще люднее:

— Ильич! Хунтик ветчинки не отвесишь?

— Ветчинкой я, брат, нонешний год, благодаря Богу, так обеспечен, так обеспечен!

— А почем?

— Дешевка!

— Хозяин! Деготь у вас хороший есть?

— Такого дегтю, любезный, у твоего деда на свадьбе не было!

— А почем?

Потеря надежды на детей и закрытие кабаков были крупными событиями в жизни Тихона Ильича. Он явно постарел, когда уже не осталось сомнений, что не быть ему отцом. Сперва он пошучивал.

— Нет-с, уж я своего добьюсь, — говорил он знакомым. — Без детей человек — не человек. Так, обсевок какой-то...

Потом даже страх стал нападать на него: что же это, — одна приспала, другая все мертвых рожает! И время последней беременности Настасьи Петровны было особенно тяжким временем. Тихон Ильич томился, злобился; Настасья Петровна тайком молилась, тайком плакала и была жалка, когда потихоньку слезала по ночам, при свете лампадки, с постели, думая, что муж спит, и начинала с трудом становиться на колени, с шепотом припадать к полу, с тоской смотреть на иконы и старчески, мучительно подниматься с колен. С детства, не решаясь даже самому себе признаться, не любил Тихон Ильич лампадок, их неверного церковного света: на всю жизнь осталась в памяти та ноябрьская ночь, когда в крохотной, кособокой хибарке в Черной Слободе тоже горела лампадка, — так смирно и ласково-грустно, — темнели тени от цепей ее, было мертвенно-тихо, на лавке, под святыми, неподвижно лежал отец, закрыв глаза, подняв острый нос и сложив на груди восковые руки, а возле него, за окошечком, завешенным красной тряпкой, с буйно-тоскливыми песнями, с воплями и не в лад орущими гармониками, проходили годные... Теперь лампадка горела постоянно.

www.almaclassics.com